SASSY IN LINGERIE

Lingerie #8

PENELOPE SKY

Hartwick Publishing

Sassy in Lingerie

Copyright © 2018 by Penelope Sky

All rights reserved.

Contents

ONE

Bones

Vanessa spent the day in her art room, pressing the tip of the brush against the canvas and getting lost in the colors of the paint. She'd been quiet lately, thinking about the conversation she'd had with her family, about the odds stacked against us.

I'd been thinking about it too.

Crow Barsetti hated me. No, he loathed me.

If there were a stronger word for hate, that would perfectly describe the way he felt.

I couldn't blame him because I felt exactly the same way about him.

That man took everything away from me, banished me to a life on the streets. He was directly responsible for turning me into the man I'd become. I had been inside his home with access to a gun, and I could have easily killed two Barsettis in two seconds. But my hatred was masked underneath the love I had for his daughter. I loved her so much I was willing to ignore his disrespect and insults. I was willing to be handcuffed like a prisoner awaiting trial.

I'd never put up with that bullshit for anyone else.

The idea of spending the foreseeable future this way, with my baby down the hall working on something she loved while I sat in my office, was exactly how I wanted to live out my life. It was peaceful, easy, and simple. Our quiet companionship was my favorite feature of our relationship. With her, I didn't have to pretend to be something I wasn't. She accepted me for exactly who I was. I never had to lie or exaggerate the truth.

That was hard to find.

And that was how I knew this was real. I accepted her exactly the same way, accepted the fact that her family may never like me. I accepted the fact that she needed to be close with her family in order to be happy—despite how much it annoyed me.

I didn't know what our next move was. Crow was putting his best men on my file, digging up every piece of dirt he could find. It was annoying because I didn't have a problem saying the truth right to his face.

Yes, I killed people—a lot of people.

Yes, I'd paid for sex. I'd paid for a lot of sex because I was into kinky shit.

Yes, I'd paid the police to look the other way.

None of those were attributes a father wanted for his daughter.

But his wife had turned her cheek to his murky past.

She'd accepted him for his criminal behavior, for the way he'd treated women in the past. She loved him despite his temper and his rage.

He and I were exactly alike.

I knew that would make him hate me more.

Max called me. "Hey, I just talked to Shane. He's doing a lot better. Went to the gym today."

"Isn't that a little soon?"

"I think he's trying to prove to Cynthia he's back on his feet again. Apparently, she's been a mess since he came home."

"I don't blame her." Vanessa had been in pain the entire time I was gone. I loved coming home to her, loved seeing the relief on her face when she saw me in one piece. It made me an asshole to say it, but I loved when she cried over me. I loved knowing her whole world would be shattered if something happened to me.

"She's trying to pull him out of the business."

That would never happen. "Shane is too deep into this. He'll never leave."

"I don't know… Cynthia wants kids."

Well, that changed everything. Being part of this life-style meant kids were impossible. Too risky. "We'll see…"

"I have another mission. Wanted to see if you wanted it."

"What about the rotation?"

"Yeah, I know," he said. "But I thought you might want it. It's in Thailand. I know you love it there."

I loved it because of the women. Brothels were on

every street, and I got my kicks before and after my missions. But now that lifestyle had been buried with my former identity. "I'll pass. I shouldn't be sent out so soon anyway."

"It's a big payout. Thirty."

I wasn't tempted by the money. "No." Vanessa was under a lot of stress at the moment. If I left, she would be pissed. She needed me right now. "I met her family earlier this week…didn't go well."

"Did you kill them?"

I chuckled. "No."

"Did they try to kill you?"

"No. Pretty nonviolent. But it was tense…they hate me."

"No surprise there."

"Said they were willing to try…whatever the fuck that means."

"Yeah." Max chuckled into the phone. "You must really love Vanessa to go through that bullshit."

"Unfortunately." Loving her gave me my greatest joy but also my greatest pain. My life was a lot simpler before she came along. Now it was turned upside down. "So, I'm going to have to pass. But let me know if you need anything."

"Sure thing." He hung up.

I tossed my phone on the table and drank my scotch, not feeling any regret for turning down the mission. It seemed like I just came back from the last one, and my account was stuffed with so much cash I didn't know what to do with it.

I looked out the window and thought about my other home in Lake Garda. Spring had arrived, so the snow was starting to melt. Tourists and adventurers would start to enjoy the lake soon. My place was still pretty isolated because of the way it was on the mountain, and I missed that peace and quiet.

I would ask Vanessa if we could go there soon since we didn't have to keep up a façade anymore.

A few minutes later, she arrived at my open door and tapped her knuckles against the hard wood. "Can I come in?"

I looked up from my drink, taking in the sight of her in my t-shirt with her hair pulled up in a messy bun. There was a spot of yellow paint on her cheek, contrasting against her dark Tuscan skin. Her arms were wrapped around her waist, and her ankles were crossed. She was barefoot, and the sight of her made me think of the nights when her feet were pressed against my bare chest. "Yes. And don't ask that again."

The corner of her mouth rose in a slight smile before she stepped inside. "I can barge in here whenever I want?"

"Always."

She moved behind me then placed her hands on my shoulders. Her fingers rubbed into my bare skin, and she massaged me the way I liked, her fingers working hard to dig as deep as possible. I liked massages that were deep and rough, penetrating the thick muscle of my frame.

I closed my eyes as I enjoyed it, loving the fact that my woman knew exactly how I liked to be touched.

When she finished, she ran her hands down my chest to my stomach. "Working hard?"

"Drinking hard."

She hooked her arm around my neck as she walked around my chair then sat in my lap. "Is that what you do all day?"

"Among other things." My arm wrapped around her waist so she wouldn't fall over, and my other hand migrated up her smooth legs. I loved every part of her body, but I particularly loved her legs. So long and toned, they felt amazing wrapped around my waist.

"Such as?"

"Work, sometimes."

"And?"

"Thinking about you. But I do that everywhere, not just in here." My hand moved up her thigh and underneath her shirt. "How's the painting going?"

"It's okay…"

I detected the sadness in her voice. "Having a hard time?"

"I guess I'm just distracted…"

I knew exactly what she was distracted by. "Don't let it bother you."

"Kinda hard to do."

I moved my face into her neck and pressed kisses

along her skin. My lips paused when I felt her artery, felt her powerful pulse. Her smell washed over me, so feminine and sexy. I could get lost in this woman at any time. I squeezed her thigh and pictured her ass in the air as I fucked her from behind. I could stare at her asshole all day. I enjoyed making love to her, but I also enjoyed fucking her like we were just a man and a woman.

She turned her head and pressed her face into my shoulder, her knees moving to her chest.

I wrapped both of my arms around her, cradling her in my protection. "I said don't let it bother you."

"Hard not to."

I wanted to tell her everything would be alright, but since I wouldn't lie to her, I couldn't say that. We both knew there was a strong chance this would end badly. There was a good probability she would leave me when her parents refused to accept me. I would go back to my empty life, and she would try to forget about the first man she ever loved.

But right now, we were still together. That was what we needed to focus on.

She pulled her face away from my neck and looked at me head on, her lids heavy with sadness. Her fingertips moved into the back of my hair as she looked at me. "Make love to me…that's the only thing that makes me feel better."

I rubbed my nose against hers, my eyes softening at her request. My lips brushed against hers, but I didn't kiss her, purposely teasing her. I loved listening to my woman ask me to be with her, so even if it wasn't exactly what I wanted, I wouldn't deny her request. I was the kind of man who would always give my woman what she wanted. "Alright."

———

VANESSA RESTED her head on my thigh while we watched TV on the couch. She'd fallen asleep, her hair stretching across my knee. She was tucked underneath a blanket, and her lips were slightly parted as she slept.

I stared at her more than the screen.

My arm rested directly underneath her tits, feeling her breathe in and out slowly. She was so much smaller than I was that sometimes I wondered if my arm was enough to crush her.

My phone started to vibrate in my sweatpants, so I pulled it out and looked at the screen. It was a number I didn't recognize, but since those numbers always seemed to be the most important in my line of work, I took it. "Bones."

A long pause ensued over the line, a stretch of silence that seemed innately purposeful. A full thirty seconds passed.

I refused to say anything more, knowing there was a person on the other line. Silence was my game, and I could handle the tension better than anyone.

"Meet me at Club Bellissima in thirty minutes. The men will bring you to the back." I knew exactly who it was even though he gave no introduction. With a deep voice full of threat, his hatred was obvious in his tone. Hearing me address myself as Bones probably pissed him off so much he needed a full minute to unclench his jaw.

"Alright."

Click.

I set the phone on the end table and looked down at Vanessa. I assumed he'd called me this late because he didn't want his daughter to be involved in this conversation. I scooped her into my arms and carried her to bed before I got dressed and left.

THE BOUNCERS at the door recognized me before I gave my name. They handed me off to another crew, and the men guided me upstairs and to the back of the bar Cane Barsetti owned. I suspected both of the brothers would be there to interrogate me.

They took me through a locked door and then into another room. With black walls and black leather sofas, it was a private room with no windows. It was soundproof and the throbbing from the bass immediately died away once I was inside.

The men shut the door behind me.

Crow Barsetti sat there alone, a bottle of scotch on the black walnut table with two glasses. He was dressed in a long-sleeved black shirt and dark jeans. His black wedding ring sat on his left hand, and his Tuscan skin was still noticeable despite the dark colors around him. His jaw was covered in thick stubble because he seemed not to have shaved since the last time I saw him. Fearless, he stared at me once I stepped inside and never once looked away.

I stepped farther into the room, noting the privacy we shared. I didn't bring a weapon to the meeting even though I had no idea what to expect. Also, the second he saw a pistol on my hip, he would immediately distrust me.

I moved to the leather sofa facing him and lowered myself into the seat. I was in a black t-shirt with black jeans, the nighttime air not bothering me. My blood was too hot, and I craved the cold. I'd left Vanessa in my bed and was grateful she didn't wake up before I left. I didn't want to explain to her where I was going, knowing she would want to come along.

Crow rested his elbows on his knees as he leaned forward, his posture suggesting his guard was down. It didn't seem like he was packing a gun, and I wasn't sure what kind of message he was trying to send to me.

I knew he didn't trust me.

He grabbed the bottle and twisted off the cap. It was aged a hundred and fifty years, so it was bound to be smooth. He poured two glasses then set it down again, the bottle thudding against the coffee table.

He grabbed his glass and took a drink.

I did the same.

He stared at me some more, his expression hardening into a look of irritation. My features alone were enough to make the bile rise up his throat, I was sure. Despite his aggression and distaste, he never pulled his gaze away.

"I'm not carrying anything. Your men checked me."

He took another drink. "Nor am I."

I couldn't stop myself from raising an eyebrow, surprised he would allow himself to be unarmed when we were alone together. He didn't trust me, but I couldn't think of a different explanation. Maybe he was trying to show respect to his daughter, but I didn't think that was the reason either.

He answered the unspoken question. "I don't need a gun to kill you. My hands will suffice."

I was much more muscular than Crow, who was ripped and lean. I packed on the muscle at a young age and never allowed it to disappear. I continued to make it grow, continued to add more weight to my workout sessions. But size wasn't always more important in a fight. He was thirty years older than me, so I had that leverage, but I wasn't arrogant enough to assume he was powerless against me. He had more experience than I did, and after all, he'd outsmarted my father many times until he died.

Eyes glued to one another, we continued to stare.

I saw Vanessa in his features, the color of his hair and skin. But I saw most of her in his presence. They were both strong, proud, and stubborn. The similarities were striking, even when they weren't in the same room together.

I didn't speak, unsure what the context of the meeting was. He wasn't there to kill me, and there was scotch on the table like we were supposed to enjoy it together. It could have been poisoned, but I drank it anyway.

"My daughter shot you." He rested his fingers on the rim of the glass but didn't take a drink. "Why?"

I was sure he'd read up on me, knew everything about me he could discover. But that was a question he would never find the answer to unless he asked me or Vanessa. As much as I wanted to lie about the beginning of my relationship with Vanessa because it was terrible, I couldn't. Men didn't respect other men who lied. It ruined their credibility. I needed Crow to respect me, even if he hated me. "Ask me anything you want, and I'll always respond with the truth. But be careful what kinds of questions you ask...because you may not want the answer."

Crow's hard expression didn't change. He didn't even blink. "Why did my daughter shoot you?"

I grabbed the glass and took a long sip, finishing the drink. I returned it to the table, letting the warm liquid burn me all the way down to my stomach. "She was trying to kill me."

"Obviously. Why?"

He didn't know about the night we met. He didn't know how long I'd kept her as a prisoner. It would hurt him to hear this story, but it would hurt more if he heard it from Vanessa. "I was working in Milan when I ran into her. I had an asshole in the alley, and she made the mistake of passing by at the worst time. She saw me kill him, and since she was a witness to the crime, I couldn't let her get away. When I went to grab her, I got a better look at her face. That's when I recognized her. That's why I didn't kill her."

Crow hung on every word, hiding his emotions behind his hard face.

"I put her in the van and drove to Lake Garda to drop the body. I left the van in the snow, carried the body to the edge of the harbor, and while I was gone, she searched the van until she found my pistol underneath my seat."

"Good," he said proudly.

I was proud too. "When I was ten feet away, she raised the gun and fired. She was aiming for my heart, but I turned and she got me in the shoulder. My feelings for her started then. I'd never met a woman who didn't flinch in the face of fear. She fought me the entire way and never gave up. She didn't hesitate before she pulled the trigger. She would have killed me without remorse if she'd hit an artery, but she didn't care. I had so much respect for her that I couldn't keep it bottled inside. She made my hands shake. She made me feel something. So I grabbed her face and kissed her." I looked her father in the eye as I answered his question, giving him the simple truth without remorse. "She kissed me back. Whatever I felt, she felt it too."

"You said she always fought you. Did she fight you before this?"

I hesitated before I answered, knowing he wouldn't take this story well. "When I tried to put her in the van in

Milan, she wouldn't go quietly. I tased her in the neck, and instead of dropping like men twice her size, she kept going. I tased her again, but that didn't stop her. She just kept going…"

His jaw clenched noticeably, his green eyes bright with hostility.

"I told you to choose your questions wisely."

"I told you I'm not afraid to kill you with my bare hands."

I knew there was nothing he wanted more. The only reason both of us were still breathing was because of our shared love for Vanessa. Neither one of us crossed the line even though she wasn't present. All we used was our words, attempting to be as civil as possible.

"I would never put a hand on her now," I said. "That's not how our relationship is. You know I'm not lying…since I'll never lie. I respect her and love her. I'd rather die than let anything happen to her. She has my full blessing to shoot me in the chest if I ever did pull a stunt like that…and I would make sure she didn't miss."

He was stoic, as if that statement meant nothing to him. "Then what happened?"

"With all due respect, sir, I don't think it matters. If I were another man, you wouldn't ask that." I hated calling him sir. It left a sour taste on my tongue. I'd never called a man that in my entire life.

"But you aren't another man. You're trash."

I took a deep breath at the insult, swallowing it as best I could without retaliating.

"Now, answer me."

"I took her to my place in Lake Garda. She had a room, food, and everything she needed."

Crow didn't ask the question that was lingering in his eyes, and I knew he would never ask it. It was every father's worse nightmare. It was so disturbing he couldn't form the words on his tongue. It was one thing for Vanessa to be tased, because she was tough and could bounce back. But to be emotionally abused against her will was another story.

So I answered it, giving him peace of mind. "I never raped her. That's not my thing. I know my father did it to your sister…but it's not the kind of guy I am. Besides, I respected her way too much to do something like that."

Crow had kept a straight face throughout the entire conversation, but this was the one time he lost control of his expression. He closed his eyes for a brief moment, a sigh of relief coming from his flared nostrils.

I averted my gaze, giving him a second to recuperate.

He poured more scotch into our glasses and took another drink, swallowing the last of his relief. "And then what?"

This was the worst part. "I told her I would kill her for revenge. I planned to tape it and send it to you. But when it came down to it…I couldn't do it. I didn't want to hurt her, not ever. It seemed like a waste, to let a woman like that leave this earth."

Crow readopted his coldness, not reacting to that piece of news. It wasn't surprising, since we were sitting there together at that very moment. "So you wanted to kill my whole family until you met her?"

I held his gaze and answered. "Yes."

"You wanted to kill my wife?" His jaw clenched a little tighter.

I nodded. "Yes."

"My son is innocent, as are my brother and his wife."

"All Barsettis are connected in my opinion. You're all the same."

"Yes," he said in agreement. "And I'm proud to say that. Perhaps you should reconsider your vengeance…"

I heard what he said, but it took a moment to grasp his meaning. "You would rather I try to kill you than watch your daughter love me?"

He nodded. "You would lose. Then you would be gone forever, and my daughter could find a better man."

His words shouldn't hurt me, but they did. He might not like me, but there was no better man out there. "I'm the best thing for her. I'm the only man strong enough to balance her power. I'm the only one who makes her feel safe. I know my resume isn't very impressive to you, but you said you wanted a powerful man who would always protect her." I pointed at my chest. "That's me, sir. Men don't look at her twice when she's with me. People are too afraid to cross me. I'm the kind of guard dog that latches on to its prey and never lets go. I'm a mountain that can't be moved. Vanessa is the kind of woman who refuses to show vulnerability and weakness. She holds her head high and takes care of herself. But with me, she *wants* me to take care of her. I'm the only man she's ever allowed to take care of her. I earned that right."

"You earned nothing. You wanted to kill her entire family. I don't know what this relationship is, but it's not love."

"Yes. It. Is." I didn't care if my words made him hate me more. I wasn't going to let him change the narrative of my relationship. "I've never loved a woman, but I know I love her. She's never loved a man, but she knows she loves me. I respect her, adore her, and would give her the entire world to make her happy. She calls me out on my bullshit, cries when I finally come home after a mission, and calls me when she's scared."

Again, it seemed like that meant nothing to him. "I made a deal with my daughter. I told her I would try to accept you, try to understand this relationship. I'm trying to like you. I'm trying to see the good in you instead of all the bullshit. But if you never get my approval…she'll end whatever the hell this is."

She hadn't told me that, but I wasn't the least bit surprised. "I'm aware of how much you mean to her. I'm aware of how important family is to her. It's the reason I'm sitting here letting you insult me repeatedly."

"I'm a man of my word. I will try. But things aren't looking good for you."

I hated knowing this man had so much power over me. He could take away the one thing that actually meant something to me. I used to care about money and women, superficial shit. But now, none of those things seemed important anymore. "Keep in mind that if you don't try hard enough, you will devastate your daughter. I know how much she loves me…because it's with the same intensity as I love her."

He brought his hands together, massaging his knuckles. "If I tell her to stop seeing you, are you going to fight for her? Turn her against me?" He showed a hint of emotion again, just the way he did earlier.

I knew how much her parents loved her. I witnessed it every time he spoke about her. I listened to the way he talked to her, like she was still his little girl even though she was a grown woman. It was the kind of love that I received from my mother when I was young, but I didn't get to cherish it as long as she did. "No. Not because I'm weak, but because I know how miserable she would be without her family. I never want to be the reason she loses the people she loves. If you felt the same way, you would be giving me a better chance than you are now."

"It's different, and you know it. Not only did your father inflict horrible crimes upon my family, but you took my daughter against her will and did terrible things to her. And you wanted to kill all of us until she changed your mind. You really expect me to accept you? To shake your fucking hand and give you my blessing?"

I knew everything was working against me. I knew my past would make this nearly impossible. The odds seemed so stacked that the likelihood of success was a billion to one. But that didn't mean I would give up—not on Vanessa. "There will never be another man out there who will love her the way I do. Not because she's unlovable, but because my love is so unbelievably fierce that it's crushing."

His eyes narrowed on my face. "You're forgetting the man who made her and raised her. You think I wouldn't die for her? That I wouldn't give her the whole world? You think my love isn't fierce? I'm sitting across from the man I despise more than anyone else on this earth— because she claims she loves you. So don't sit there and pretend your love is stronger than mine—her father's."

"That's not what I meant, sir."

He spoke through clenched teeth. "Seemed like it."

"You should trust your daughter. She's a very smart woman. She wouldn't have fallen in love with me without reason, especially after everything we've been through. She didn't want to love me. She wanted to forget me. It's like she doesn't have a choice, that's how strong our bond is. Trust her."

"Love is the destruction of reason. She's obviously not thinking clearly right now."

"And she's not supposed to. Did your wife think clearly when she fell in love with you?" I shouldn't cross the line into his personal life, but I had to.

Both of his eyebrows rose, like the head of a rattlesnake that had just been provoked.

"I know you took Pearl from my father for vengeance. I know you held her as a prisoner against her will. I know you made her work for her freedom by making her—"

"Shut. Up." The vein in his forehead throbbed, and

his face tinted with redness. His jaw was tighter than I'd ever seen it. "Don't talk about my wife. You can talk about me, but leave her out of it. She's off-limits."

I'd already made my point anyway. "Your relationship didn't start under the best circumstances. That's all I'm trying to say. But was she wrong for falling in love with you? Does that mean you aren't the right man for her? No. Vanessa and I aren't any different. In fact, our stories are so similar, it's strange."

"Does my daughter know all of this?" he asked, his voice breaking.

"No…" I'd mentioned some things, but never extensively.

"I don't want her to know. You understand me?"

I nodded. "She knows that you and your brother have been criminals in the past. She knows that your relationship with her mother is shrouded in mystery because you never talk about it, and I think she can connect the dots on her own. But I've never explicitly told her how it started and how you treated her."

He nodded.

"But she does know what my father did to her mother…" I knew Vanessa didn't want them to know, but he'd asked me a direct question and I couldn't lie.

His eyes shifted down to his hands. He went rigid, his chest tight because he'd stopped breathing. Heartbeats passed, and he didn't move. Then he brought his hands together at his lips and closed his eyes. "Fuck." He rose to his feet and paced around the room, his hands on his hips. "Fuck." He stopped on the other side of the room and faced the wall, his back rising and falling quickly. "You told her?"

"I thought she knew…"

"What did she say?"

"Nothing. She cried."

He crossed his arms over his chest, releasing another deep sigh.

"She didn't want you to know she knew. She knows it would hurt her mother. But she wishes she could be there for her…talk to her about it. She doesn't think less of her…she's just heartbroken over it. She told me she hated me even though I wasn't guilty of the crime. That was another hurdle for us, but she overcame it. I don't want you to think Vanessa fell in love with me immediately. It took a long time, and even when she did, she did her best to fight it. She always told me she would never love someone who would hurt her family. She didn't want this to happen. Neither did I."

Crow didn't turn around, his breathing still uneven. "Leave." His tone held finality, the closure to the conversation.

I grabbed my glass and finished the rest of it, not wanting it to go to waste. I walked to the door without saying another word, knowing Crow hardly respected me as a human being. Once I opened the door, the sound of the music from the club surged in.

"Griffin."

I turned back around, noting the way he chose to address me.

"Don't tell her you told me. We'll talk to her about it...when the time is right."

I nodded even though he couldn't see me. "Of course."

TWO

Vanessa
———

I had fifteen paintings in my collection.

I should take them to the winery to be displayed, but asking my parents for help didn't seem appropriate right now.

There was this distance between us, as if an ocean separated us rather than a few hundred miles. I hated the way it felt, to be closed off from the people I was closest to. I suspected they hadn't told Conway or anyone else yet. Otherwise, Conway and Sapphire would be calling me right now.

Inspiration didn't come to me that afternoon, so I didn't work in the art room.

I moped around the house all day while Bones worked in his office.

I hated being patient. I hated waiting to know the outcome of this nightmare. It didn't seem like it could ever work, but then again, I hadn't believed my parents could be so understanding of it this far.

So maybe anything was possible.

I went back into our bedroom and opened my drawers. Inside were different lingerie options, some I'd already worn and others I hadn't touched. I picked a purple one and put it on before I walked to his office.

When I was most upset, I turned to Bones for reassurance. When he was buried between my legs with his lips pressed against my ear, I wasn't afraid of anything. All I thought about was him, the way he told me he loved me when he made love to me. That was what I wanted now, a distraction, so I wouldn't think about the pain in my life.

I stepped in the entryway and looked at him sitting behind his desk, his broad shoulders powerful. Ink ran all over his chest and shoulders, highlighting the impressive muscles underneath the skin. His deadliness was beautiful; his eyes drops of beauty in a sea of terror.

He slowly looked at me from top to bottom as he sat behind his desk, studying the purple push-up bra and matching thong. I was barefoot because he liked me that way. The color went well with my skin tone, and he'd always been attracted to the dark color of my skin.

His eyes slowly made their way back up to mine, his face hard with devastating masculine features. His hard jaw was a stark line in comparison to his neck and shoulders. His jaw was cleanly shaven from his shower that morning, revealing the fair skin I liked to kiss.

He rose from his chair and walked toward me, his

sweatpants low on his hips and his chest bare. He pressed me against the frame of the doorway and angled his neck down to kiss me. His hands immediately went to my tits, and he squeezed them, his large palms aggressive.

I breathed into his mouth, feeling the bumps form on my skin at his touch. The second we were connected, I forgot about the turmoil in our lives. I only thought about the man I loved, the mountain that protected me from the wind and the rain.

He lifted me into the air with a single arm and pulled me to his chest as he carried me to the bedroom. His mouth was still on mine, never breaking our kiss as he moved me into the other room.

He laid me on the bed and dropped his sweatpants and boxers to reveal his impressive dick. "You want me to make love to you, baby?" He widened my legs then pressed kisses to the insides of my thighs, his soft lips devouring my sensitive skin.

I arched my back and ran my fingers through my hair as I felt him kiss me. "I want you to kiss me…"

"Where?" He inched his mouth closer to the apex of my thighs, knowing exactly what I wanted.

"You know where…"

"Tell me." He kissed the skin right next to my panties, not going any closer.

I growled through my teeth then pushed my panties down my body, wanting me to be available to his mouth. "Here."

He pulled my panties off the rest of the way then

lowered himself onto the bed, scooping his hands around my thighs and holding himself on his elbows. He pressed a kiss to my aching clitoris before he began.

My head rolled back, and I moaned in pleasure. "Yes…right there."

He circled my nub with his tongue, his warm breath escaping across my folds. He sucked and kissed the area before his tongue dived into my slit, adding his saliva to my already weeping arousal.

"Griffin…" No man had ever done this to me, and I didn't understand how amazing it could feel until he put his mouth there.

"You want to come, baby? Or you want to wait for me?"

I wanted to wait, but I didn't think I could. I was too deep into this, too deep into how good it felt. If I had to stop, I'd cry. "Make me come…"

He was rougher with me, sucking and biting my clit with aggression. He stimulated me harder and deeper, his tongue doing amazing things just like his dick could. He pushed hard until I was on the edge, about to explode in a fiery wave of pleasure.

Then he gave it to me, providing me one of the greatest highs I'd ever experienced.

Without thinking, I grabbed his face and pulled him harder into me, my hips bucking against him as I got off to his amazing mouth. I could feel his hard jaw against me, and that made it even better. It felt so good I knew I needed to give him an amazing blow job as a thank you.

"God…yes." I ran my hand through my hair as I closed my eyes, treasuring the memory of that satisfying orgasm.

He pulled his mouth away and held himself on top of me, his lips shining with the evidence of my arousal. "You like that, baby?" He kissed my stomach and moved his lips along my rib cage.

"Yes."

"Has a man ever done that to you?"

"No."

"Good thing I was your first. You would have been disappointed by the others." He grabbed my hips and dragged me to the edge of the bed so his cock could press against my wet folds. He prepared to slide inside me.

"Wait." I pressed my hands against his rock-hard abs.

"Yes, baby?" He ground his cock against my folds, his throbbing length created the perfect friction against my swollen clit.

"How do you want me?"

His eyes narrowed in interest. "In every way imaginable."

"You know what I mean. How do you want to give me your come?"

His eyes darkened, like I'd said the perfect words to get his engine revving. His hands released my hips, and he moved up the bed until he was against the headboard. His long cock rested against his stomach. He beckoned me to him with a slight nod of his head.

I straddled his hips and gripped his shoulders, crawling on a mountain of solid rock. I kept my bra on, my tits pressed tightly together with a noticeable line of cleavage between them. I looked into his eyes, seeing the same arousal I'd just felt when his mouth was between my legs.

He hooked his arm around my waist and pulled me up slightly as he pointed his cock to my entrance. Then he nudged me down, making me slide all the way until his entire length was inside me.

I felt my body tighten around him, his large size stretching me wide apart. It always took time for my body to accommodate him. He was a monster compared to my petiteness. My arms wrapped around his neck, and I pressed my forehead to his while I sat on his lap, being claimed by his throbbing dick.

He gripped my ass with his big hands and kissed the corner of my mouth. "Nice and slow, baby." He pulled me up by my cheeks, directing me up and down his length. His mouth moved to my neck, and he kissed me softly, his lips trailing over my pulse and everywhere else. He thrust up slightly, giving me his length at the same speed I lowered myself onto him.

"You never like it slow."

He pressed his mouth to my ear and breathed into my canal, his hot breaths showing his arousal. "I do with you."

BONES ASKED ME TO DINNER, so we got dressed up and went to a nice place down the road.

Going out for a meal wasn't really our thing.

But since we weren't hiding anymore, there was no reason why we couldn't.

I wore a little black dress, and he wore black slacks with a dark blue collared shirt. He hardly dressed up, so when he did, he looked delicious. His broad shoulders looked even wider in the fitted fabric, and seeing his shirt tucked into his tight slacks showed off the firmness and hardness of his physique.

There was one drawback to going out.

I couldn't stop staring at him—but that was true for everyone else too.

We both had a glass of wine with dinner, and instead of scanning the people in the restaurant, Bones stared at me with his soulful blue eyes. Head slightly tilted and his fingers on his glass, he looked at me like we were completely alone inside that restaurant.

I was used to the look, but I never got tired of it. "Why do we go out if we do the exact same thing at home?"

"I like to show you off."

"You hate it when men stare at me."

"But I like watching them turn away when they see me with you." Innately arrogant, he lifted the corner of his mouth in a smile. "Besides, it's nice not to cook once in a while."

"Is that a jab at me?" I asked.

"It wouldn't kill you to open a cookbook."

My eyes narrowed, but I didn't glare at him because I knew he was being playful. "I'm an artist, not a chef."

"And I'm a killer, but I manage to do both."

It shocked me he made that confession out loud in a public place. He really wasn't scared of anyone. I sipped my wine and watched the waiter set our dishes in front of us. Bones always ordered something boring, like fish and greens. I got pasta because there was nothing better in the world than hot noodles, sauce, and cheese. "My parents haven't called me, and it's been over a week. I guess I should call them tomorrow." Bones and I hadn't talked about that day since it happened. We spent our time pretending there was nothing wrong.

He dropped his look and drank from his glass.

I caught the movement. "Why do I feel like you know something?"

He shrugged and returned his wine to the table. "Maybe I do."

"And what would that be?"

He held my gaze for a long time before he answered. "Your father called me the other night. We went to Bellissima and had a good talk."

I almost dropped my glass. "Where was I?"

"Asleep."

"Why didn't you tell me this until now?"

"There's really nothing to talk about."

"Uh, I disagree. I want to know everything."

Like this was completely casual, he picked up his fork

and dug into his salad. "It was a conversation between men, baby. He asked me a lot of questions, drilled into me like an enemy, and we parted ways with the same mutual dislike."

My heart fell into my stomach even though his words weren't the least bit surprising. "So, he's made no progress in accepting you?"

"No, not really."

I crossed my arms over my chest and sighed.

"And this is why I didn't want to mention it."

Now our evening together was ruined, and I didn't have an appetite. A delicious meal was placed in front of me, but all I could think about was the tense conversation my father had with the man I loved.

Bones glanced down at my food. "Eat. Otherwise, you're just going to watch me eat." He stuck his fork into his salmon and took a bite, his angular jaw moving as he chewed. There was nothing he did that wasn't sexy. Every movement he made exuded masculinity.

I wasn't going to let this delicious dinner go to waste, so I stuck my fork into the pasta and forced myself to eat. Once the cheese and sauce hit my tongue, my appetite returned. I hadn't been exercising as much since I'd shacked up with Bones so now I had a bit of a tummy, but the food was so good I didn't care. And Bones didn't seem to mind the weight I'd put on. "He told me he would try…" I should change the subject, but I couldn't.

"He said the same to me."

"Does it seem like he is?"

Bones chewed his food thoroughly before he swallowed. "Yes. He wouldn't have talked to me for an hour otherwise."

"What did he ask you?"

He kept eating his dinner, taking his time as if I hadn't just asked him a question. "How we met. How our relationship started. Things like that."

"And did you tell him?"

"The whole truth and nothing but the truth."

"You're serious?" I asked in shock.

He nodded. "I told your father I would never lie to him, and because of that, I told him to seriously consider his questions before he asked them. He might not want the answers. But he asked them anyway."

"So you told him you tased me?"

He nodded.

"And he was just fine with that?"

"No...he was pretty angry. But he didn't strike me. He didn't hesitate to insult me though...called me trash. I think that's his nickname for me." He brushed off the conversation like it wasn't as intense as it really was.

"And you told him you were going to kill me?"

He nodded. "Yeah. But I also told him you're such an incredible woman that the last thing I ever wanted to do was hurt you...so I didn't. He knew you shot me, and I told him that only made me respect you more. I told him you're the kind of woman who turned me into a man. All I want to do is protect you, and I would take a bullet for you in a heartbeat."

"Did you tell him you asked me to sleep with you to keep my family safe?" There was no way my father would look the other way on that one.

"No. But I told him I never raped you. He got a little emotional at that part."

I couldn't even imagine how that made him feel. Something like that happening to me was his worst nightmare.

"I told him everything he wanted to know without holding back. But I also reminded him that none of that matters because that's not how we are now. You never wanted to love me and did your best not to. This isn't something that either of us can control. I told him I was the perfect man for you because I could protect you and provide for you. I would do anything for you, die for you. I emphasized all of that because that's what's most important right now. But truth be told, I don't think he's ever going to look past everything else...not that I blame him."

"Yeah..."

"I told him I wouldn't stand in the way if he doesn't approve of me. If we can't make this work, I'll bow out. I wouldn't ever ruin your relationship with your family. I understand how much they mean to you."

My eyes softened, the guilt hurting my chest. My father obviously told Bones about the deal he'd made with me.

"I meant what I said, and I hope that makes him understand how much I love you...because I'm willing to lose everything for you to be happy." His eyes moved down to his plate as he kept eating.

I took a deep breath, feeling twinges of pain inside my chest. Bones was a remarkable man, selfless and loving. "You saying that should be enough for my father to accept you."

He kept eating, his eyes downcast.

"We're not going to lose, Griffin. This is going to work."

He finished the food on his plate, taking the final bites until his plate was clean. He hadn't looked at me yet, like he was tuning out everything I just said. He grabbed his wine and took a long drink, his throat shifting as he swallowed.

"I'll make it work, alright?"

He set his glass down and looked at me, his blue eyes unreadable. "Baby, I'll do my best to get your father to accept me. But I'm not going to change who I am to make him like me more. And you're going to have to accept the fact that there's a good chance this won't happen. Your father has to look past a lot of crimes I've committed, my family history, along with everything else. It would be unrealistic to expect him to be okay with all of that. I'm not going to get my hopes up. Neither should you."

"Please don't say that…" I'd never been happier in my life than I was with Griffin. I loved sharing his bed every night. I loved seeing him first thing in the morning. I loved making love to him, feeling his powerful body sink me into the mattress. I'd never felt this way about anyone else. I didn't want just to live in the present with him, but share my entire lifetime at his side. Losing him was something I couldn't even contemplate. "I can't live without you."

His expression didn't change, his eyes just as stern as they were before. "Yes, you can, baby. Don't forget how strong you are."

"I'm stronger when I'm with you."

His blue eyes showed his unbreakable power, the way he kept his emotions bottled deep inside even when he was upset.

"You act like my father's decision has already been made."

"Because it has," he said simply. "I want to enjoy the rest of the time I have with you. But we both know how this is going to end."

Tears welled up in my eyes. "You're supposed to fight for me…"

"Why do you think I continue to let your father call me trash? Every time I stop myself from punching him in the face, I'm fighting for you. But I'm not going to come between you and your family. I love you too much to do that. You can always find another man. You can't find another father or mother. Treasure them while you have them…because they'll be gone before you know it."

"I don't want another man, Griffin. I want you." I quickly wiped the tears away, not wanting them to ruin my makeup when we were in public. "I'm never going to love anyone the way I love you."

"You're going to have to try." He turned his gaze away, looking at everyone sitting in the restaurant.

I kept my emotions in check, but only barely. My heart was breaking, and I felt sick to my stomach. Bones predicted the end of this relationship, and the fact that he was probably right made me incredibly weak. I couldn't lose my family, but the idea of moving on from him and trying to find someone else to love was sickening. What we had was a love that couldn't be described. It was powerful, beautiful, rare. I didn't want to let it go. Not now.

Not ever.

I LOCKED my ankles together around his waist and held on to the back of his neck as he thrust inside me, pushing me hard into the mattress as his large dick hit me in the right spot over and over.

He breathed into my ear, his arousal coming out as sexy pants.

I squeezed his hips with my thighs as I dragged my nails down his back. Once we'd walked in the door, he slipped off my heels and took me to bed. He made love to me without my having to ask, knowing I wanted him just like this.

I needed him just like this.

"Griffin…" My fingers moved through his hair, and I moaned toward the ceiling.

"Baby." He lifted himself so he could look down at me, his expression hard and sexy. With blue eyes the color of the ocean, he looked at me like I was his paradise. He thrust into me hard but made his strokes nice and slow, trying to make this last as long as possible. Without blinking, he kept his gaze on me, like I was the sexiest thing in the world. It was the same look he gave me every hour of the day, but when he was deep inside me, it was more intense.

I never wanted him to give that look to anyone else.

The idea of him moving on with someone else caused me so much pain.

I wanted him all to myself. I never wanted to share. "I love you…" My hands gripped his shoulders as I felt his thickness stretch me wide apart.

He rocked into me nice and unhurriedly, making my toes curl because it was just as good slow as it was fast. He was an enormous man who covered me completely like a blanket, the sweat from his chest dripping onto my chest as he moved. Even when he did all the work, he never seemed to mind. He just enjoyed being deep between my legs, conquering me on his bed while I confessed just how deeply I loved him. "I love you too, baby."

I cupped his cheek and kissed him, and our lips moved together with the same passion as other parts of our bodies. I breathed into his mouth and let out a moan, feeling the chemistry ignite between us. When I had all of

37

him, it was always my breaking point. It was always the moment that pushed me over the edge. "Right there…"

He gave me his tongue and thrust into me a little harder, keeping his kiss going at the same time. He gave it to me deep, hitting my clit with the perfect amount of friction. "Come all over my dick, baby."

I was already sheathing him in all of my cream, all of my arousal. My hands wrapped around his body, and my nails anchored into his back. I moaned against his mouth, exploding around his dick as I lost my breath. "Yes…"

He watched my performance, his eyes focusing on my open mouth as well as my eyes. "So. Fucking. Beautiful." His eyes darkened in intensity as he watched me finish, his cock thickening slightly inside me as he reached his trigger.

I grabbed his ass and pulled him deeper. "Come inside me."

He gave his final pumps before he released, groaning as his cock twitched with pleasure. He dumped everything inside me, filling me with his heavy seed. It exploded inside me, warm and with significant weight. I'd never let a man come inside me before Griffin, and now I understood just how good it felt. But I suspected it wouldn't have felt so good with anyone else.

He kept kissing me even when he was finished, his cock slowly softening inside me. It was one of those nights when the sex didn't seem to end. We kept wanting more, wanting to treasure every moment we had with each other because this relationship could be over tomorrow. I wanted to be stuffed with his come, to have his seed spill out on the sheets once he pulled out.

"You like taking my come even more than I like giving it," he whispered against my mouth.

"Yes. Every drop."

I WAS SITTING in the art room drinking wine when my mom called me.

I hadn't talked to her since that afternoon at the house. There was a heavy silence between us, an awkwardness neither one of us wanted to address. I'd never felt so distant from her, like another conversation could destroy what little connection we had left.

I answered. "Hey, Mama."

"Hey, sweetheart." She spoke the same words as she did before, but her tone was certainly different. "What are you doing?"

"Painting and drinking wine."

"That sounds like a nice afternoon."

My man was down the hall, and I wore his baggy shirt as I worked. It was definitely nice. "It is. I actually have a lot of paintings I need to give to you."

"How many?"

"About fifteen."

"Wow, that is a lot," she said. "But I know they'll sell. You seem to get better with every piece."

"My technique does seem to get a little stronger." I

wasn't sure if she was going to bring up Bones or not. I wasn't sure if I was going to either. The afternoon had been a nightmare and both of us wanted to forget about it.

"Your father and I are in town for work. Thought we could get dinner or something."

Was the invite just for me? Or both of us? "Yeah, that would be nice."

"Are you guys free around seven?"

So he was invited. "Yeah."

"You want to meet us there? I can text you the address."

"Sounds good to me."

"Alright. See you then, sweetheart."

"Mom?" I knew how hard this was for her. She was trying so hard to pretend everything was normal, but she detested this situation as much as my father did. She just did a better job of hiding it.

"Yeah?"

"Thanks…for trying. It means a lot to me." The thought of losing Bones made me realize how much he meant to me. I didn't want to say goodbye. I'd already done that once, and it didn't work. Every man after him wouldn't compare. I might get married someday, but in the back of my mind, I would always know my husband was second-best.

"Of course. Your painting expressed everything you've never told me with words."

I knew it expressed the depth of my emotion, the

powerful love that sank all the way down to my bones. "I'll see you soon."

I WORE tight jeans with a white top and a black sweater. Black booties were on my feet, and I had a gray scarf around my neck. Spring had arrived, but it wasn't exactly warm yet. That evening in particular, there was a strong breeze filled with the coldness of old snow.

Bones wore black slacks and a gray collared shirt, his dress clothes fitting his muscular body to a T. With sculpted arms, narrow hips, and a tight stomach, he looked undeniably handsome. Even when his ink was hidden, he had a profound appearance of deadliness. He exuded terror, a persona no one crossed. He wore a nice watch that I only saw him wear when he got dressed up, and his dress shoes were so shiny because he hardly ever wore them.

I knew he went the extra mile for me.

We stepped inside the elevator and rode it to the lobby. Bones didn't show his displeasure over our dinner plans even though he was probably dreading them. Anytime he was with my father, he turned into a punching bag for insults.

I looked at him, seeing him display the same indifferent exterior he always had plastered on his face. "Thanks for doing this…"

The doors opened, and he stepped out first. "Don't overthink it."

"Overthink it? This is going to be just as shitty as last time."

"Then there's no reason to stress about it. We know what's gonna happen." We got into his truck then headed down the road. The restaurant we were going to was close by. It was a nice place, but more on the casual side of the spectrum. It was a restaurant we'd never been to before, and I suspected that was because my father wanted to go to a place where he didn't know the owner.

The closer we got to the restaurant, the more my heart started to palpitate. My palms were sweaty and cold at the same time. Nothing would happen tonight that was worse than what had already happened, but there was so much at risk.

My happiness.

I needed my family to accept him, but unless I held a gun to their head and forced them, I didn't think it was possible.

Bones parked the truck in the parking lot then turned to me. "You need to relax, baby."

"I didn't say anything," I said defensively.

"You don't need to say anything to tell me how you feel. You're wound up so tight you might snap in half." He grabbed my hand and brought it to his lips to kiss it. "Be yourself. Talk to them the way you normally do. The more casual you make it, the easier it'll be for them."

"My father doesn't like casual. He likes intensity as much as you do."

"But your mother doesn't. While your father is the head of the household, she calls all the shots. If she wants me to stay, she has the power to make it happen. Remember that."

"But she's probably the one more likely to say no…" She'd been the victim of his father when she was my age. It was the kind of suffering you didn't just forget about.

"Women are more compassionate than men. But she's also more logical than your father. She can separate emotional thinking from logical thinking."

"You gathered all of this from being around them a few times?"

He shrugged. "They're pretty easy to read. One thing is clear…they're a team. Your father might be the only one in the room with me sometimes, but he definitely discusses everything with her. After all, she was the one who killed my father. I've been told she stashed a knife inside her stitches, and then when she was alone with him, she ripped the knife out and stabbed him to death."

My jaw dropped. "Jesus Christ…"

He nodded.

"Fucking badass."

Bones didn't crack a smile, probably because his father was the victim of the situation. He didn't get mad about it either, understanding my family had every right to do what they did. "My father actually captured your uncle. Held him captive and asked to switch him for your mom. Crow wouldn't do it, obviously. Your mother made the switch behind his back. She saved your uncle and killed my father all on her own."

I knew my mother was a strong woman, but I had no grasp of her true bravery. She willingly went back to her former tormentor to save my father's brother. She killed him on her own—with no one's help. I knew exactly where my strongest qualities came from, but now I was even more proud of them. "Wow…"

"Point is, she has as much power in the decision as he does."

"But you've never tried talking to her."

"Like your father wants me anywhere near her. That would cross the line. I would call her or stop by for a private conversation, but that would piss off your father so much that it would be counterproductive."

When it came to my mother, my father did turn into a guard dog.

"Let's go." He killed the engine, and we hopped out of the truck.

Bones didn't hold my hand or show me any kind of affection. All he did was open the door for me, and to anyone watching us, we would seem like two people who hardly knew each other—not lovers.

My parents had a table in the corner, with significant space around it as if it was a table they gave to customers who required a lot of privacy. The other tables were filled with families and couples enjoying wine and their dinner.

Bones let me walk first, and I headed to the table with

dread in my heart. My father didn't even look at me because he was too busy staring at Bones, like he suspected my lover would make a sudden movement and kill everyone in the restaurant.

It made me sick.

My mother rose from her seat and greeted me with a hug. Nothing could stop her from smiling at me, regardless of how she felt about the man standing behind me. Her eyes glowed with happiness anytime she looked at me, like she always missed me—no matter what our circumstances were. "Hey, sweetheart."

"Hey, Mama."

She squeezed my arm before she stepped aside so I could greet my father. She looked at Bones like she didn't know what to do. She stared at him with her blue eyes, examining him not with hatred but reluctance. "I feel rude not shaking your hand, but I'm just not ready for that yet…"

Bones didn't seem the least bit offended. "I understand."

My father hugged me next, embracing me the way he always did. He squeezed me and kissed me on the forehead, treasuring me with his unconditional love. He hated the man I was sleeping with and thought I was stupid for being with him, but that would never change the way he felt about me. "*Tesoro*, you look nice."

"Thanks, Father."

When my father looked at Bones, his affection disappeared instantly. The only greeting he gave Bones was a cold look.

Bones didn't wait for the handshake that wasn't coming. He pulled out the chair so I could sit down and took a seat in the other chair.

"It's nice to see both of you," Bones said politely.

My father stared at him like he'd just heard an insult instead of a greeting.

My mother was the only one who could say something back. "Thank you." She grabbed her menu and looked down at it.

Bones didn't seem to care about the cold response. He would normally have his arm resting on the back of my chair or his hand on my thigh, but he didn't do either of those things. He kept his hands in his lap, taking up as little space as possible. He was by far the most handsome man in the room, gorgeous from head to toe. If I weren't so involved in the situation, I would be pissed about all the women making eyes at him.

My father sat directly across from Bones with the menu in his hands. He barely looked at the menu for more than a few seconds before he looked at Bones again, like he might miss something important.

Things seemed to be getting worse rather than better.

"What are you getting?" I asked Bones as I held my menu for him to read.

"Salmon."

"You always eat fish."

He shrugged. "I like it."

"Well, I'm getting the lasagna." I shut my menu then grabbed a piece of bread from the basket.

"Good choice," he said.

My mother shut her menu then grabbed her glass of red wine. "So…how are you?" There was no good way to break the ice between all of us. This was a terrible situation, uncomfortable for everyone.

"Good," I answered. "I've been working on my artwork. Griffin has been working in his office a lot."

"Are you painting at his place?" Mom asked quizzically.

A part of me wanted to lie, but I knew we had to be honest about everything. "Griffin made me an art studio at his place. It has a large window that overlooks the city, and it has the perfect morning light. It has enough room for all my supplies."

"Oh, that's nice," Mom said. "That explains how you can fit all those paintings somewhere."

My father set down his menu and stared at Bones without blinking.

Bones held his gaze, maintaining the standoff.

God, this was bad.

"Are you two living together?" Mom asked, her eyebrow raised.

"No," I said quickly. "I just spend a lot of time there. After the whole thing with Knuckles, my apartment has never felt the same."

My father's eyes shifted to me. "Why didn't you tell

me that? I could have gotten you a better place. I could have bought you anything you wanted—"

"I didn't tell you because I knew that was exactly what you would say." I said quickly. "I don't want your money, Father. I've already taken enough from you."

"I don't mind giving it to you, *tesoro*," he said. "I would much rather you take my money than stay with trash like him."

I respected my father's anger, but I was getting fed up with the insults. "Stop talking to him like—"

"Let it go," Bones said. "It's fine. He can call me whatever he wants."

"And I will." My father clenched his jaw. "And I can get you a new place to stay."

"It's not just about the place," I said. "I just like knowing…" I didn't finish my sentence, not wanting to share anything too intimate that would make the conversation even more tense. "He makes me feel safe. I already said that."

"Conway is right down the road," my father said. "You can stay with him."

"He's getting married and has a baby on the way," I said. "He doesn't want me there."

"Then find another guy," my father countered. "A better one, and one who isn't a murderer."

Bones kept a straight face, taking all of this with no reaction. He was the kind of man who shut down insults before they were even uttered. He wasn't afraid to cause a scene or tell someone off. But he kept his silence—for me.

"Father, stop," I said, keeping my voice low because we were in public. "I don't need a man to take care of me or make me feel safe. That's not the purpose of having someone. But Griffin makes me feel invincible, like nothing could ever hurt me. I'm not afraid of someone coming through the front door to hurt me because he would never let that happen. Just the way you make Mom feel safe, I feel safe with him. And I don't feel that way with just anyone."

"You don't feel safe with me?" my father asked. "My whole life, all I've done is keep you safe. I'm telling you now, I don't like the man you've chosen, and I don't trust him. But now, you don't listen to me."

"It's not the same thing, and you know it," I said quietly. "And you told me you would try, but it doesn't seem like you're putting in any effort at all. The second you look at him, it's like we're starting over from the beginning again. We need to move forward, make progress. This man means everything to me. I want this to work…I need it to work." I didn't want to get emotional in the restaurant, but my eyes were welling up with tears.

Bones turned toward me. "Vanessa, it'll be alright." He kept his voice quiet, so quiet I wasn't sure if anyone else could hear it.

"I've already told you that I would leave him if we couldn't get past this," I said, ignoring Bones's attempt to calm me down. "I've already shown you how much you mean to me, even if that hurts Griffin. Now you need to meet me halfway. You aren't even trying. All you do is insult him over and over, and it needs to stop."

My father didn't show a hint of remorse. "I told you I wouldn't be nice to him."

"And that's fine with me," Bones said. "Let it go, Vanessa. I told you I'm bulletproof."

My father's gaze shifted back to him, the anger still heavy.

I ran my fingers through my hair, my insides ripped apart. "Just try. You said you would, and you aren't."

My mother turned to my father. "She's right, Crow."

My father breathed through his flared nostrils, irritated.

"We need to uphold our end of the deal," my mother said. "Insulting him and ignoring him don't qualify."

"What do you want me to say?" my father demanded. "You want me to ask about work? Have fun killing people this week? Or you want me to ask about his family? About his rapist father and his whore mother?"

Bones took a deep breath, the insult piercing him.

"Father." I glared at him. "Leave his mom out of it. She had nothing to do with anything that happened to us."

"She fucked my enemy," my father said. "So she's my enemy."

I hated my father like this. I hated his cruelty. I didn't even recognize him anymore.

My mom rested her hand on his shoulder. "Crow—"

My father pushed his chair back as he stood up. He

50

stormed out of the restaurant, obviously having no intention of returning. He weaved through the tables then disappeared out the entryway.

None of us moved.

Mom didn't go after him.

I wanted to cry. I wanted to sob to myself like there was no one around.

Bones stood up next.

"What are you doing?" I asked.

"Have dinner with your mother." He pushed his chair in and walked behind me. "I'll talk to your dad."

"Just leave him alone," I said. "You can't talk to him like this."

He leaned down toward me, one hand on the table. "Watch me." He kissed my temple before he walked away and left the restaurant.

I turned back to my mom, my eyes still wet. "I hate this…I hate this so fucking much."

My mother gave me a look of pity, a sadness in her eyes and her frown. "I know you aren't used to seeing your father like this. It's been a while since I've seen him behave this way. It's as if he's returned to thirty years in the past. His life of peace has been disturbed, and he can't stand it."

"Well, it's the first time in my life I've been happy, and I don't want to lose it."

"You've been happy before, sweetheart."

"Not like this." I stared at the flickering candle between us. "Mom, I love him. I know he's the worst possible person I could pick, but it's how I feel. I'll never love anyone else the way I love him. I wish you understood that…"

She watched me, her blue eyes gentle. "I do understand, Vanessa. I can see it written all over your face. I can see it expressed in your artwork. I can see the depth of your feelings and the complicated layers surrounding it. It's not that I don't understand. Sometimes, we can't choose who we love."

"Then why can't you guys just accept him?"

"Vanessa, while you may love him with all your heart, it's difficult to expect us to forget everything we've been through. It was before your time, so it's hard for you to comprehend, but his father did many terrible things to us…"

My heart broke when I imagined what that man had done to my mother. "But he's not him. You're punishing him for something he didn't do."

"Up until he met you, he didn't seem to be that different."

"But he is different. He would never hurt me or any of you."

"You're right," she said. "He probably wouldn't. But you're asking us to welcome a man into our family that we despise. Remember, who you marry is who we marry. He will be a son to your father. He is the last man your father wants to have as a son, the son of his greatest enemy."

"Let's not skip to marriage just yet," I said. "I just want you to accept the fact that I'm dating him."

"Are you telling me you don't want to marry him?" She raised an eyebrow. "Because if this isn't serious, then it's not worth our heartache."

"Yes, I do want to marry him." I didn't want to say the words out loud because it would make losing him more painful. "I want a family and a life together. There's probably someone out there better suited for me, but I don't want that person. I want him."

She sighed quietly under her breath.

"I'm begging you."

She looked away, as if she couldn't handle my emotion.

"He said he would let me go if you didn't approve of him. If that's not a declaration of true love, then what is?"

"I'm not denying that he loves you. He wouldn't put up with your father if he didn't. He obviously doesn't scare easily, and I respect him for that. He's fighting for you, taking insults when he would normally kill the man who issued them. But you're asking us to love him too… and I'm not sure if we can."

"You said you would try," I whispered. "You aren't trying."

"I know." She closed her eyes for a brief moment. "You're right. It's hard to try when the only thing connecting us is something we don't speak of. The name Bones hasn't been said in our home for thirty years. Your father forbade anyone from saying that name. And now the door to our past has reopened, and it seems like we'll never escape it."

"Maybe you aren't supposed to escape it. Maybe this is the closure everyone needs. What better way to end the blood war for good than to welcome him into our family?"

My mother didn't give a response, her lips pressed together tightly.

"You told me Father wasn't perfect. He was cold and cruel. You said he wasn't easy to love and he refused to love you. It sounds like he wasn't much better than Bones. He did criminal things for a living. He's killed people too. Maybe I don't understand the full story, but it sounds to me like our stories are extremely similar. But you loved Father, and I see how much he loves you every day. How is it any different?"

She didn't answer, staring at me with a guarded gaze.

"How is it any different?" I repeated.

"It just is, Vanessa."

Silence settled between us, the quiet full of discomfort. She tucked her hair behind her ear, her button wedding ring catching the light. "We will try to overcome this, Vanessa. We'll try harder. Don't expect this to happen overnight. It'll take time."

"That's fine," I said. "But anytime you're in the same room together, all Father does is yell at him."

"I know," she said quietly. "I'll talk to him about that…again. He can't see straight when it comes to you.

He gets very emotional and aggressive. He's so angry because he loves you so deeply, but he's also trying to make this work because he loves you so deeply. He's at war with himself, and he has no control over it."

"Yeah…I can see that."

She placed her hand on mine. "I want you to be happy. I really do."

"I know, Mama…"

"Just be patient with us. It seems like Griffin is more than patient with us."

"He'll do anything for me. It wasn't easy for him to let go of his hate. It took a long time. But he finally did it, so I know he understands it'll take you a while to feel the same. I would just like it if we could be in the same room without…everything going to shit."

"Me too," she said. "Maybe we'll get there eventually."

"Yeah…maybe."

THREE

Bones
———————

I left the restaurant and stepped out into the cool night air. My collared shirt was uncomfortable because it was stiff like cardboard. My slacks weren't my favorite either; nothing compared to my jeans. I only put on this ridiculous outfit to make a decent impression on her parents.

Which didn't happen.

Crow had crossed the parking lot, and now he was headed to a bar across the street. Of course, he wouldn't leave his wife far behind, wanting to be easily accessible at all times. But he didn't want to sit in there with me a moment longer.

Too bad I wasn't better company.

I followed him and walked into the bar. It was quiet because not too many people were drinking on a Wednesday. He sat at the bar, an empty glass in front of him. Only a few amber drops were left behind, evidence of the scotch he just downed. He got the attention of the bartender and asked for another.

I took the seat beside him.

He must have detected me before I joined him because he didn't react to my company.

"I'll have the same."

The bartender slid the drink toward me.

I didn't pick it up, choosing to watch him in my periphery. The time I spent with Crow taught me a lot about him, about the way he thought, about the man he was behind the information I'd gathered about him. I'd dug up every piece of information I could, but I never uncovered the depth of his feelings for his family.

For his daughter.

Conflicted, he couldn't stop hating me, but he also couldn't order Vanessa to stop seeing me. Every time he took a step forward, he took another step back. His love and hate balanced him out, bringing him to a painful stalemate.

I respected him for the way he loved Vanessa, for the way he wore his heart on his sleeve whenever he was around her. He wasn't afraid to show weakness, absolutely unashamed to love with all his heart. That was a sign of a truly powerful man, of someone so invincible that perceived weaknesses didn't make him weak at all. "Tell me what to do."

He stared straight ahead.

"Tell me what you want from me. I'll do it."

He rested his fingertips against his lips. "Disappear."

I didn't feel the pain from his insult, even though he meant the word with every fiber of his being. "If I disappear, Vanessa will suffer."

"Yes. But she won't suffer forever."

"But she'll never find a man who will make her forget about me. You don't see it, but what we have is real. I can hear her when she doesn't speak. I can feel her pain as if it's my own. Loving her is like having my heart exist outside my body. She's taken everything from me, and I've willingly given her everything she's asked for. Give me a chance to love, protect, and honor your daughter. I'm not the kind of man to ask for acceptance or approval. If someone doesn't like me, I don't give a damn. You're the last man I thought I would ever work so hard to prove myself to. But here I am, practically on my knees, doing whatever it takes to make this work. Because I will take whatever insult you throw my way so I can have Vanessa. If you want to beat me to within an inch of my life, fine. If you want to shoot me, go ahead. Whatever you want, I'll do it."

"My hatred for you goes behind the flesh, *Bones*."

"Then hurt me in some other way. I don't care."

"The best way to accomplish that is to take my daughter away from you…and I'm very tempted."

"That wouldn't hurt me," I whispered. "That would kill me."

He finally turned my way, his green eyes boring into mine.

"Don't question my love for her. You have every right

to hate me. I would judge you if you didn't. But my love for her is genuine. I don't want her for any other reason. Women are plentiful to me, whether I pay for them or find them in a bar. Vanessa gives me something no other woman ever has. She gives me something I can't live without. I would do right by her, always be faithful to her, and make her a very rich woman."

He stared into his full glass again. "I'm not blind to the fact that my daughter is beautiful, smart, and full of so much life that she's a beacon that can be seen miles away. You aren't the only man who would fall madly in love with her. She could have anyone she wanted. It just baffles me that she wants you."

"I'm not that bad, Crow."

"Not that bad?" he asked with a scoff. "You're my worst fucking nightmare."

"I'm not my father."

"But you want to be," he spat.

"Not anymore. I'm Griffin—just Griffin."

"You told me the terrible things you did to my daughter."

"And I left out all the good things I've done for her."

He turned on his stool, facing me with his elbow on the bar. With a challenging gaze, he asked, "Then tell me, what have you done for her?"

After every terrible thing I did to her, I made up for it by being the man she could always rely on. I was always there for her, even if she couldn't see me. "She acts like she doesn't need someone to take care of her, and for the most part, that's true. But I know she wants a man who can handle her. That's me. I always watch her, even when she thinks I'm not looking. She tried to push me away and get rid of me because she despised me, so she went out, drank too much, and walked home alone in the dark."

Crow's nostrils flared slightly, and his eyes filled with disappointment.

"Some guys pulled over to the side of the road, did some catcalling, and when she told them to fuck off, they got out of the car to grab her. But I was there, watching her. I stepped out of the shadows and scared the boys away with a simple look. Then I picked her up and carried her the rest of the way home. She's a smart woman who doesn't usually put herself in stupid situations like that, but she was so upset with me she wasn't thinking clearly. But I was there for her. I'm always there for her."

Crow kept his fingers around his glass but didn't take a drink.

"She said she didn't want to see me anymore, and I respected her decision. But I knew she didn't feel safe in that apartment anymore, not when I wasn't there. So I parked my truck at the curb during the night so I could keep an eye on her place. She eventually called me because she was scared, kept hearing noises in the apartment. When I told her I was outside, she was finally able to get some sleep."

Crow still didn't say anything.

"She's not the kind of woman who ever needs anything, but she's not afraid to need things from me. That's because she trusts me, wants me to take care of her. I need you to let me do that."

Crow drank from his glass.

It didn't seem to matter what I said, he would continue to hate me. "I'm not going to downplay my hatred for you. I've wanted revenge for a long time, my bitterness only growing during my tenure on the streets. You took everything away from me, and it didn't seem fair. I was subjected to a cruel existence, while you got to have the perfect family in a damn mansion. I wanted to kill all of you for taking away my inheritance. Letting that grudge go was the hardest thing I've ever had to do. But when Vanessa asked me, I couldn't say no. I couldn't deny what she wanted more than anything in the world. It was a hard sacrifice to make, to drop the blood feud. I know that's not impressive to you because that's the very reason you hate me, but I let the past go—for her. You can't question my love for her or my honesty. I will say the truth to your face, no matter how painful it is."

"Is that supposed to impress me? You're a terrible man, but since you're honest, that makes you a good one?" He swirled the liquid in his glass before he took another drink. "Still trash, if you ask me."

I hated my new nickname. "I offered to buy her a gallery where she could display her pieces. I was the one who encouraged her to drop out of school because she's too talented to listen to some bullshit instructor act like he knows better than she does. I've urged her to pursue her dreams because she's meant for greatness. I don't hold her back. I push her to her full potential."

He drank from his glass again.

"There's nothing more I can say or do to prove myself to you, Crow. You just need to acknowledge everything I've said."

He slammed his glass down. "You expect me to look the other way when you say you wanted to kill my wife?" He turned his gaze back to me, cold and fiery. His arms were flexed with blood, muscle, and adrenaline. "My son? My brother? I should just let that go since you don't want to kill my family anymore? Water under the bridge?"

"It's better than holding on to a past that has no relevance now. Yes, I was your enemy. I'm not anymore."

"And if Vanessa leaves you for another man, I'm just supposed to assume that my family is still safe? All you have to do is change your mind, and all our necks are on the line."

"She wouldn't leave me for someone else." I was the only man she wanted, and I would love her so fiercely she would never want anyone else. I knew how to please a woman, and now I knew how to love one. "Trust me on that."

"You have no idea what the future holds. Vanessa might wake up one morning and realize you aren't what she wants anymore. She might not be able to overcome what you do for a living. You don't know. And then, my family would be vulnerable. You would know everything about us, our every weakness. I can't let that happen."

"I promised Vanessa I would never hurt her family, regardless of what happens between us. I'm a man of my word—and I keep my promises."

"Honorable men keep their promises. But you aren't an honorable man. You know exactly what you are…"

Trash. "I already know how this is going to end. You aren't going to be able to accept me—even though it'll break her heart."

He stared straight ahead. "You're probably right. So why don't you just give up?"

"Because I'm not going to give up until I absolutely have to. She means too much to me, and I know how much it'll kill her if she loses me. My entire life rests in your hands—and I hate knowing you have this much power over me."

He drank his scotch, his elbows resting on the table.

"Just keep in mind your relationship with your wife. If her family had told her not to be with you, because you were a criminal and a murderer, what would you have done? Where would you be right now? And where would she be? Would she be better off without you? Or did you give her everything that she deserved?"

He didn't acknowledge my words, continuing to stare straight ahead.

"I know you don't like me, but I'm the best thing for her, Crow."

He gripped his glass, his knuckles flexing like he was considering smashing it. "I've sacrificed everything for my family. My brother and I live peaceful lives in the countryside, where we make wine and mind our own business. I don't want my daughter getting involved in that lifestyle, the kind of world I've tried to protect her from."

"I keep my business separate from my personal life."

He shook his head. "Not possible. You cross the wrong person, and they never stop coming after you. And you might not realize it until it's too late. As long as you do that for a living, the risk will always be there. And Vanessa is the first person they'll use against you—just how you tried to use her against me."

"I would never let that happen."

"It's out of your control. There are so many things I don't like about you…but I despise your ignorance and arrogance the most." He finished his glass then left cash on the bar. "I'm done talking to you." He left me at the bar and walked out.

I stayed on the stool and didn't go after him, unsure if this conversation had helped or just made it worse.

VANESSA and I were quiet on the drive home. She didn't tell me what happened with her mother, and I didn't mention the conversation I had with her father. Judging by our silence, we both knew nothing good happened on either front.

We took the elevator to the top floor and went straight to bed. I considered what Crow said, that my criminal lifestyle could catch up with me and hurt Vanessa in the end. She asked me to stop working, but without my job, I wouldn't have any other purpose. It was a business I'd been running a long time. I couldn't just walk away from it.

Crow never asked me to.

It made me realize he was never going to give me a real chance. If he were, he would have asked if I would quit the business and retire. The sacrifice would speak volumes, and then he wouldn't be able to hold it against me.

So he didn't ask at all since it wouldn't make a difference anyway.

I didn't tell Vanessa because it would only make her upset.

We went to bed, and I lay on my back in the center of the mattress. After a night like that, I wasn't exactly in the mood for sex. I always wanted Vanessa, but the overwhelming sense of frustration burned out my drive. The time I had with her seemed shorter and shorter every time I spoke to her father.

The situation was like a bomb ready to go off.

When it did, Vanessa would be gone.

Vanessa moved on top of my body and lay directly on my chest. She was in my t-shirt with her hair spread everywhere. She was too upset to remember to take off her makeup, so she kept it on as she lay on top of me. She immediately closed her eyes with her hands resting on my warm skin, clinging to me like it was our last night together.

She still didn't mention dinner, and neither did I.

We were both too depressed to say anything.

THE NEXT FEW days were spent in silence.

We hardly spoke to each other, neither one of us wanting to address the dead space between us. We coexisted without speaking, making love regularly and having our meals together. But the conversation had dried up, like muttering a single word would destroy us both.

I felt like I'd failed her.

I wondered if there was something else I could have done or said to persuade her father, but I knew there was nothing. He was a stubborn man, set in his ways. The good things I did for his daughter didn't outweigh the bad. I might protect her, but it didn't diminish the risk our relationship brought to the table.

She lay beside me one night, her leg hitched over my hip as her arm curled around my torso. Her head rested beside me on the pillow, her beautiful face not as pretty because she was so sad. I could see it in her green eyes, the way her eyes didn't emit as much light.

My fingers trailed up her arm and then stopped at her

neck, feeling her steady pulse. I'd made love to her the way she liked, but the connection between us wasn't as strong as it used to be. The sadness we both shared had dampened our chemistry, had masked the pleasure because we were scared we would lose each other.

"I don't know what to do…" She stared at my chest, her eyes downcast on purpose. "Every time we're with them, it's like it's the first time. They're just as angry as the day I brought you home. My mom said she would talk to my father and they would work on it…but I don't know."

I knew she didn't want to talk about this, but the silence over the last few days had been too much for her. It was eating away at her, piece by piece. "We need to be patient."

"I don't mind being patient. But it seems like they aren't even trying."

"They don't know where to begin."

"I understand that…but all my father does is insult you."

"I can handle it, baby. Don't worry about that."

"That's not the point. I can't stand to listen to him talk to you that way…it hurts me."

I tugged her closer to me and kissed her on the mouth, making her feel better with my kiss.

"I told my mom how much you mean to me…that we have to make this work. I need you to be happy. She seemed to listen. Her eyes light up so brightly every time she sees me because she misses me so much. I see it every single time. I know how much she loves me. I know how much she wants me to be happy. I'm just not sure if that will be enough."

I recognized the look Vanessa had mentioned, but I saw it on both of her parents' faces. Vanessa was the center of their universe, and anytime they got to be with her, it brought them such joy. I knew they hated being five hours away from her. I knew they wanted to spend more time with her.

That gave me an idea—even though I didn't like it. "Baby?"

"What?"

"What if we got a place in Tuscany? Somewhere close by?"

Her eyes didn't soften in hope. "You know I would love that. But I don't want to plan for the future right now…it'll just make it harder."

"I meant now. Your parents love seeing you. So what if we got a place down there, and they got to see you all the time? We could show them what it would be like if they accepted this relationship. It would make them happy, even if that sense of joy has nothing to do with me. I could go to the winery and help out, spend time with them every day even if we don't talk much. It might work."

"You would do that?"

She shouldn't be surprised. "I've already put up with a lot. You know my love has no limit."

"But what about work?"

"I don't have to be in Milan. If I get called out for a mission, I'll fly out of Florence."

"Where would we live?"

"I'm sure we could rent a house nearby."

She moved her hand to my chest, a touched expression in her eyes. "Well, I would love to do that, but I don't want to ask you to do something you don't want to do."

"You didn't ask me. I offered."

"I know, but…"

"This is the only thing I can think of. Unless you have a better idea."

"I don't."

"Then let's do it." I didn't want to be five hours away from home. I didn't want to see her parents every day while I helped out at their winery. I didn't want to be insulted and called trash on a daily basis.

But I wanted this woman so damn bad.

Finally, a smile formed on her lips as she moved closer into me. "Thank you." She wrapped her arm around my neck and kissed me, her soft lips aggressive against mine. "Thank you."

———

VANESSA DIDN'T HEAR from her parents for the rest of the week, and by the time the following Monday arrived, I'd found a villa for us to rent just a few miles away from the Barsetti mansion. It was a short-term rental and already furnished, and that was perfect for us since this experiment wouldn't last long.

Even if her parents finally got on board, we wouldn't live in that rental. We'd return to Milan and my penthouse on the top floor. I liked that building because it gave me all the space I needed, along with privacy and powerful fortifications. In the center of the city, people were always around, so it made it difficult for anyone to touch it. For a man like me, it was the perfect place to live.

But out in the middle of Tuscany, there was nothing. Just soil, fields, and vineyards. The only reason I found it beautiful was because Vanessa incorporated the landscape into most of her paintings. The place was special inside her heart—because it was where she grew up.

We pulled up to the house then explored the inside.

"It's nice." Vanessa examined the living room and kitchen, seeing the Tuscan-style furniture that was in the photos online. Her eyes kept moving to the open windows and to the green fields that stretched beyond.

I couldn't help but hate this place. Wide open with nothing surrounding it, it was like being in a gunfight completely naked. There was no protection or cover. Anyone could approach the property from the front or behind.

Thankfully, this was only for a few months.

Vanessa turned back to me when she picked up on my mood. "You don't like it."

I glanced around, not caring about the nice furniture or the big TV on the wall. "Not my style."

"You might change your mind."

I was even less likely to do that than her father. The soldier inside me was constantly on the lookout for an attack. I hadn't told anyone I was coming here, so it would be virtually impossible to find me. Even Max didn't know what I was up to. "Have you told them?"

"No."

"Then this is going to be a big surprise." Her parents would be thrilled Vanessa was close by, but then their happiness would be thwarted by the inked murderer she came with. Despite my handsome features, my overall appearance didn't aid in my efforts to get them to accept me. I was a terrifying man covered in formidable tattoos. I looked the same on the outside as I did on the inside— like a murderer.

"Yeah…" She crossed her arms over her chest. "But I think they'll be happy about it…for the most part."

They would only be happy when I wasn't in the room. "I'll unload the truck."

"I'll help you."

"I got it," I said quickly. "I'll bring everything in, and you'll unpack it."

"Sounds like a good setup."

AFTER BEING THERE for a few days, we finally made our move.

We drove to the winery with her paintings in the bed of the truck. The winery was ten minutes away, and the entire drive was spent with a scenic view. Spring had infiltrated the land, and the bright sun cast the fields in a golden hue.

Vanessa could hardly sit still because she was both nervous and excited.

We pulled down the windy road toward the entryway of the winery, cobblestone making up the Tuscan-style buildings. The land was full of flowers and trees with the iconic look of an Italian winery. Past the buildings was the rest of the property, vineyards that stretched out endlessly in the distance.

I parked the truck and killed the engine.

A black sports car was parked beside us. A flashy car wasn't Crow's style, so I assumed it belonged to his brother. I hadn't interacted with Cane much since I first came to the house, but I suspected he hated me as much as his brother did.

Vanessa stared at the view outside the window, infatuated by the place she'd spent her childhood. Ever since we came to Tuscany, her eyes lit up a little more than usual. Being home made her undeniably happy. I was surprised she ever left in the first place.

"Ready?"

She nodded before she got out of the truck. She came

around to my side then grabbed my hand as she headed to the entrance.

I dropped her hand, giving her a slight shake of my head. Her father didn't like it when I called her baby, so he definitely wasn't going to like watching me hold her hand. It would irritate him, so it was best not to do it.

We walked down the hallway and met Crow's assistant, an older woman who looked like she was approaching retirement. She let us go to Crow's office without warning him, knowing Crow would want to see his daughter no matter what he was doing.

Vanessa tapped her knuckles on the door before she opened it. "Hey, are you busy right now?"

Crow sat behind his desk, his hands pressed together with his fingers resting against his lips. A glass of scotch was in front of him. Cane was there too, drinking with him, probably discussing their mutual hatred for me. But the second Crow laid eyes on his daughter, he lowered his hands, and like I wasn't standing right behind her, the affectionate glow entered his face. As if time had stopped, she was the only thing in the world that mattered to him. "No. *Tesoro*, I'm never busy when it comes to you." He rose to his feet and came around the desk to hug her. He wrapped his thick arms around her and squeezed, his chin resting on her head. Fatherly love was in his eyes, and even though she was a grown woman, he still held her like she was a child. "I'm always happy to see you."

Cane stood up next and smiled at her. "Hey, sweet-heart." He hugged her next, his affection matching his brother's. "What a nice surprise. I'm tired of doing all the work around here."

Crow looked at me next, and all the joy drained from his face instantly. I was the storm in summer, the hurricane that would destroy his whole life. I was nothing but a nuisance to him, the evil that couldn't be defeated. I'd seen that look of hatred in every man I killed, but none of them hated me as much as he did—even though I'd claimed their lives.

Cane stared at me just as coldly, like he couldn't stand the sight of me.

I wasn't intimidated by either one of them, but my faith in this plan started to disappear. "It's nice to see you both." I could say nothing else, but something needed to be said to break the tension.

"It'd be a lot nicer if you were dead." Cane was a lot more aggressive than his brother, thinking emotionally rather than logically. He was both loyal to his brother and protective of his niece, so he wanted nothing more than to cause me pain.

"Uncle Cane." Vanessa stared at him with sheer disappointment. "Don't say that to him."

"Why?" Cane kept his eyes on me. "I mean it."

Crow didn't intervene, letting his brother say whatever he wanted.

His insult didn't mean anything to me. I was bullet-proof, so words bounced off even better than actual bullets.

"I mean it too," Vanessa hissed. "He's done nothing

but work his ass off—"

"And before he was doing that, he was working his ass off to kill us," Cane snapped. "So yes, I wish he were dead. I wish he were dead because a piece of trash like this asshole doesn't deserve you." He turned to her, his eyes full of anger.

Vanessa was turning red in the face, about to explode. "I'm sick of this. I'm tired of you talking to him that way. In the beginning, I understood. But it's been almost a month, and you're still treating him like dirt."

"He is dirt," Cane snapped. "I'd spit on him right now if you wouldn't throw a tantrum about it."

Crow watched me without blinking, as if I might lose my temper and strike his brother.

If I laid a hand on either one of them, I would never be able to take it back. I had to absorb their rage and keep a stoic face at the same time.

"I mean it." Vanessa moved in front of me, placing her petite frame between them and me like that would do anything. "Father, you told me you would try. Keep talking to him like that, and I'll walk out. If you won't hold up your end of the deal, I won't hold up mine."

Crow finally looked at his daughter again, a slight hint of panic in his eyes.

"I didn't make any deal," Cane said. "So if I want to do this—" He pulled his hand back and slugged me hard in the face, throwing as much force behind it as he could. "I will."

I knew it was coming, but I didn't stop it, letting his

fist hit me in the nose and eye. I hardly turned with the punch and didn't react at all, proving that I was stronger than both of them combined.

Vanessa covered her mouth and shrieked. "Oh my god!"

I turned back to Cane, my jaw clenched with anger, not pain. "That the best you got?"

Cane's eyes narrowed, and he pulled his arm back again.

"Hit me as many times as you want." I was letting my temper get the best of me, but I couldn't control it anymore. "You're going to do more damage to your fist than you are to my face. I'm harder than stone, harder than anything you can throw at me. So if you want to break your hand against my face, be my fucking guest."

Cane punched me again, hitting me in the jaw.

I didn't react again, proving he didn't have any power over me.

"Stop it!" Tears flooded her eyes, and she pressed herself against me, her hands cupping my face to check my injuries. "I'm so sorry. Are you alright?"

I grabbed her wrists and gently pulled her hands from my face, my eyes on Cane and not her. "You're hurting her, not me."

That seemed to mean something to Cane, because he lowered his hand.

Vanessa turned back to her uncle. "Don't do that ever again. I mean it. I'll cover him with my body if I have to."

Cane kept his eyes on me. "I'll kill this fucking asshole—"

"Cane." Crow silenced him with just his name. "I hate him too, but no more."

I knew he didn't intervene for Cane or me. He did it for Vanessa, who was still on the verge of tears.

Vanessa turned back to me and buried her face in my chest, her arms hugging my torso. She breathed against me, doing her best to control the emotions that were chaotic inside her heart. She knew I was fine, that I could take pain far worse than this, but letting me be treated this way was killing her. It broke her heart to see her family hate me so viciously, attack me so ruthlessly.

I hated listening to her cry. It killed me. I used to be indifferent to it, but when she was in pain, I was in pain. My hand moved under the fall of her hair, and I cradled her against me. "Baby, it's alright."

"No, it's not…" She sniffed against me then walked out of the room, unable to look at any of us anymore.

I stayed behind, watching both men immediately look guilty for what had just happened. They didn't give a damn about me, but they felt like shit for hurting Vanessa. Cane clenched his jaw and sighed. Crow crossed his arms over his chest and leaned against the desk.

I didn't wait for an apology or some form of reconciliation. "Vanessa and I rented a villa a few miles away from you. She wants to be closer to you, and I'd like to help out around here. I don't know shit about wine, but I can move heavy stuff."

Crow couldn't stop himself from raising his right eyebrow. "You moved here?"

"Not permanently," I said. "She just wants to be close to you for a while. Spend more time with you. And I'd like to get to know you better. Or better yet, let you get to know me. Give me something to do around here, or I'll find something."

"Didn't realize you were an ass-kisser," Cane spat.

If he were anyone else, he'd be on the floor choking on his own blood. "You took your wife from Tristan and made her sleep with you so she wouldn't have to go back to the man who beat and hurt her."

The second I mentioned his wife, Cane's eyes narrowed.

"Now she's your wife, and your in-laws live right down the road. Both of you are acting like you're better than me, but we're exactly the same. We're equals. So get off your fucking high horse and take a look in the mirror. We're all murderers and criminals here."

"But Vanessa is not your equal," Crow said. "She's not our equal either. She's above all of us."

I didn't have an argument against that. "If putting up with your bullshit makes me an ass-kisser, that's fine with me. I'm only here for Vanessa. I've come to terms with the fact that you'll never like me, but don't expect that to hurt my feelings. I'll do anything to make this work for her, even withstand your punches and ridicule. For the last month, all you've done is disrespect me, insult me, and now hit me. It's not gonna scare me off. Nothing is going to scare me off. I'm unbreakable and untouchable. I'm stronger than both of you combined. I've killed members of the mafia and even the leaders of small countries. This is child's play for me. I can handle anything you throw at me. So maybe you should stop with the strong-arm tactics and just try to see the way I love her. Because that's all that matters—that I'm in love with Vanessa and I would lay down my life for her. You would do the same for your wives. We're the same. Like it or not—we're the same."

FOUR

Vanessa

I sat on the cobblestone patio with the uninterrupted view of the vineyards. I snatched a bottle of wine out of the cellar and enjoyed it alone, sitting in the sunlight as the breeze moved through my hair.

It kept getting worse. Now they were hitting Bones.

I knew this would be difficult, but damn, this was ridiculous.

Footsteps sounded behind me, but I didn't turn around to see who it was. If they thought they were getting some of my wine, they were wrong. My hand tightened on the neck of the bottle, claiming it as my own poison.

My father pulled out the chair across from me and sat down.

He didn't throw the punch, but I was still angry with him.

Uncle Cane came next, falling into the chair beside me.

I ignored them both, being ice-cold. I kept drinking, my sunglasses covering my swollen eyes. Bones could take any hit, but it still broke my heart to see my family treat him that way. He didn't deserve it.

My father sighed. "Vanessa—"

"Don't say you're trying because you aren't trying," I snapped. "We moved here, and Griffin is willing to spend more time with you at the winery. He's willing to do anything to make this work, even let you punch him in the face." My gaze turned to Uncle Cane. "I'm disappointed in both of you. I know you're stubborn and prideful, but your minds are so clouded by hatred that you're continuing a war you could bring to an end. I love this man, and despite everything he's doing to be accepted by you, you continue to disrespect him— continue to hurt me. I don't want to hear an apology or an excuse." I slammed the bottle down and rose out of my seat. "When we come here tomorrow, you will give him work to do around the winery, and I'll work on my paintings. You will treat him like a human being, not a punching bag. Do you understand me?" I'd never told off my father or uncle like this before, but they had it coming. Both of my hands went to my hips as I stared at them, my sunglasses blocking my ruthless stare.

My father was quiet.

Uncle Cane stared straight ahead.

"Do you understand me?" I repeated.

My father clenched his jaw before he spoke. "Yes, I understand."

I turned to Uncle Cane.

He stayed quiet.

"Uncle Cane," I pressed.

He rubbed the scruff on the side of his face. "Got it."

"And you will apologize to him."

Uncle Cane looked at me, his eyes incredulous. "Over my dead body."

"Cane," I hissed. "What you did was wrong. He restrained himself for me, but you can't do the same for me."

"I'll never apologize for what I did," Uncle Cane barked. "But I'll apologize to you...and make sure it doesn't happen again. That's the best I can do." He faced forward again before he grabbed the bottle and took a drink.

That was good enough for me. "Good." I snatched the bottle out of his hand and walked away.

"Vanessa." Uncle Cane turned around in his seat.

"What?" I stopped and turned around, but I didn't walk back to the table.

"Did you tell him anything about us?" he asked. "About me and your aunt?"

I didn't know there was anything to tell. "I don't know what you mean."

"He knows a lot about me," Uncle Cane said. "I'm just wondering if he got that information from you."

Bones told me my uncle was in the Skull Kings and

had a criminal background. But he hadn't said anything more than that. "No. He already knew about both of you when we met. I've never shared any personal information about your lives with him…I would never do that." I turned around again and walked away. Even if they said something else to me, I wouldn't turn back.

I'd had enough for the day.

HIS EYES HAD TURNED black by the time we got home.

"Let's put some ice on it." I opened the freezer in the kitchen and picked up a few ice cubes.

Bones yanked my hand out of the freezer and shut the door. "It doesn't need ice."

"Yes, it does. It looks terrible." I placed the ice in a towel and wrapped the cloth around the cubes before I rose on my tiptoes and placed it against his eye. I stared at the stark discoloration, the bruising, and the swelling. He was the strongest man I'd ever known, but seeing him in any kind of pain broke my heart. I wanted to cry all over again.

He stared at me, his blue eyes not showing any relief at the touch of the ice cubes. He looked at me in pity, like I was the one in pain instead of him. "I don't need it, baby."

"I don't want it to get worse."

"It won't." He grabbed my wrist and gently pulled my hand away. "This is nothing but a scratch."

"Half of your eye is swollen…"

"And in a few days, it'll be back to normal." He grabbed the cloth wrap from my hand and set it on the kitchen island. "If you really want to make me feel better, I have something else in mind." His arm hugged the curve of my back, and he pulled me closer to him. His neck bent down to look at me, his hard jaw kissable.

I pressed my face against his chest. "I'm so sorry…"

"Don't be. Let it go." He rested his chin on my head. "You're underestimating me."

"That's not it. I'm just so hurt my family would do that to you…"

"Cane is a lot more impulsive than Crow. His actions didn't surprise me."

"Doesn't matter," I said with a sigh. "It hurts me that they would do that…hurt the man I love."

"They don't see me that way, baby. They see me as my father's son, not the man you love. I'm their enemy, and they can't look past that. They're soldiers, so their guards are always up. Don't take it so hard. They're just trying to protect their family. I don't blame them for that."

"Doesn't give them the right to hit you."

"I'm glad they did."

I lifted my gaze to look at him. "Why?"

"Show them what I'm made of. Show them how much I can take. Show them that they can press my buttons all they want, and I still won't cave. They may not like me, but they'll respect me—eventually. In a man's world, respect is everything." His fingers moved underneath my chin, and he stared at my lips. "So let this go. You know what I'm made of. The only thing they could possibly do to hurt me is take you away from me…and we have to make sure that doesn't happen."

My fingers wrapped around his wrists as I looked into his hard eyes. "I know. But that's easier said than done…"

"We'll take it one day at a time, starting tomorrow." He swiped the pad of his thumb across my bottom lip, his callused skin rough compared to mine. His eyes darkened as he looked at me, his thoughts no longer on my family. "You still want to make me feel better?"

"Always."

He dropped his hand and walked into the living room where three large couches surrounded a coffee table. He dropped his jeans and boxers and pushed them to his ankles before he sat down, his large cock resting against his stomach. "On your knees." He rested both arms over the back of the couch, taking up as much space as possible like an entitled king.

His arrogance never surprised me.

His eye was slightly swollen and discolored from the bruise, but somehow, the injury only made him look sexier. He could take any kind of pain without being affected by it. Stone-cold and rock-hard, he was as impenetrable as a cliff face.

He snapped his fingers then pointed to the ground at his feet.

I raised an eyebrow, surprised by his crassness. "Bold, huh?"

"Yes. But I think I earned it." He nodded to the ground again.

I didn't mind getting on my knees for this man at all. I was happy to do it. But I would never take orders from anyone, not even him. Disobedience was in my blood, along with stubbornness.

His cock thickened the longer he waited, like he enjoyed this standoff. He got off to my temper, to my resilience. He'd been that way since the night he met me, wanting to get me to submit—and loving every time he failed.

His shirt was still on, covering his muscles and tattoos, but his corded neck and tight forearms hinted at everything underneath the cotton shirt. He was over two hundred pounds of solid muscle, probably two-fifty. He ate more protein in a single meal than I ate all day.

"Take off your shirt."

The corner of his mouth rose in a smile before he cooperated. He pulled it over his head and tossed it onto the armrest. "Better?"

"Yes." I sank to my knees, my hands sliding up his muscled thighs.

He took a deep breath as I kneeled, his eyes immediately narrowing as I positioned myself in between his thighs. He watched my fingers move up to his hips, my nails digging into his skin.

He grabbed my shirt and pulled it over my head,

messing up my hair as he dragged it free of my body. The straps of my bra came next, and he pushed them down until my bra fell around my torso.

I reached behind me, and I unclasped it so it could fall to the ground.

Bones stared at my tits, his eyes drinking them in like he didn't see them every single day. His look was so manly, so territorial, that I never wanted another man to look at me like that. Nothing made me feel more beautiful than when he claimed me with just his gaze. He reached both hands out and palmed my breasts, rubbing his thumb across the nipples as they started to harden. "I love these tits." He pinched my nipples slightly, making my breathing hitch. He grabbed the back of my neck and guided my lips down to his length.

I moved with him, aroused by the heat in his gaze. My lips pressed against his sac, and I kissed the textured skin, my tongue feeling the special grooves. His fingers rested under the fall of my hair, and he watched me, studying the way I kissed his balls. "Suck."

I drew one into my mouth, ran my tongue every-where, and then released it.

He moaned in approval.

I did the same to the other before I dragged my tongue along his base, right over the thick vein that lined his entire shaft. I moved to the tip and licked away the drop that formed on the crown.

My hand gripped his base and directed him to the ceiling so I could push my throat down his length. I moved as far as I could go before I felt the need to gag and then pulled back again. My throat was sore from the stretch, and my mouth produced more saliva to sheathe him everywhere.

Bones moaned again, telling me enjoyed it. "Nice and slow."

He wanted this to last, to enjoy the sight as well as the sensation. Just like when I asked him to make love to me, he gave me exactly what I desired. He seemed turned on by the way I told him what I wanted without any shame. Now he did the same to me, telling me to suck his dick good without making him come.

I moved slowly, taking his cock over and over while massaging his balls at the same time. On my knees in front of the couch while my panties started to soak from my arousal, I knew I was in the exact position most women wanted to be. They wanted to be pleasing a man like him, who was handsome, strong, rich, and powerful.

But I was the only one who had the privilege.

"Fuck, you're good at that." He wrapped his hand around my hair, fisting it like the reins of a horse.

I dripped my saliva all down his length, getting him soaked and slick. My tongue tasted every drop of arousal he gave, and I could feel him getting thicker and thicker. I did my best to make it last, but it seemed like he was enjoying it too much. "Your dick tastes good."

His eyes immediately darkened, and he gave a slight, involuntary tug on my hair. "Fuck, baby."

I pulled him out of my mouth and locked eyes with him as I dragged my tongue from his base to his tip again.

He clenched his jaw, like he was pissed I was making this feel so good. He grabbed my neck and pulled my mouth away from his dick. Then he brought me farther in between his legs as he gripped himself by the base. "I'm gonna fuck those tits."

I'd never done that before.

He leaned forward and dragged his tongue up the valley between my breasts, kissing me and laving me everywhere with his tongue. He breathed hard against me, gripping me around the rib cage with crushing force.

I closed my eyes and breathed, loving the way he grabbed on to me so ruthlessly.

He pulled away and then brought my palms to each side of my tits. Then he sandwiched his dick in between them, his wet cock sliding against my soaked flesh. Both wet from each other's kisses, we fit perfectly together. My boobs were on the smaller size because I was barely a B cup, and his dick was enormous in comparison to my petiteness. I was slightly embarrassed, knowing this would work much better if I had a bigger rack.

But he didn't seem to care how small my tits were. He cupped my hands and guided me up and down, making my tits squeeze his length as I moved. He closed his eyes for a brief moment, like he was overcome by how good it felt.

Now I didn't feel so self-conscious anymore.

His hand moved to my neck, and he guided me at the

pace he wanted, our slick bodies making sex sounds as they moved together. He pressed his big feet against the floor, moving his hips up to push his dick through my slick tits. He bent his head over the back of the couch for a second, releasing a masculine moan that shook the walls. "Jesus Christ, I'm gonna come all over those tits." He looked at me again then grabbed himself by the shaft. He jerked himself hard, coming a second later across my wet flesh. He moaned loudly, the white drops creating a huge puddle across my tits and in the valley between my boobs.

Watching him come so deeply made me want to come just as hard. I felt my pussy tighten in arousal, wanting the thick cock pointed at me. His come was so heavy and so warm, and staring down the barrel made me wish that come was inside me as well as all over me.

He finished seconds later, his eyes full of satisfaction. He stared at his handiwork like he was proud of what he'd just accomplished, getting so much come all over me that it started to slide down right away. White, heavy, and scalding hot, it stuck to my skin like thick drops of glue. The only reason why it began to slide was because it was so heavy. "Gorgeous fucking tits."

My hands snaked up his thighs, and I watched his dick slowly soften after his pleasure had erupted across his entire body. I licked my lips and stared at him with a plea in my eyes.

He grabbed me by the neck and pulled me toward him, getting me off my knees and onto the couch. He undid my jeans and pushed everything down, making me naked from the waist down. He pulled me into his lap and pressed his fingers between my legs, finding my throbbing clit and my soaked pussy. "You really liked sucking my dick." His arm wrapped around my waist, and he pulled me against his chest, smearing his come across his body as well as mine. He kissed me hard on the mouth, crushing his lips against mine as his fingers moved through my slit and his thumb rubbed my clit.

"I love sucking your dick," I said against his mouth.

He paused as he breathed, his fingers halting for a short moment so he could moan, and then he started to kiss me again. His thumb rubbed harder, and his fingers fucked me faster. "Jesus Christ, baby."

My nails clawed at his shoulders, and I ground against his fingers, feeling the pleasure start almost immediately. I was so hard up that just a simple touch was enough to send me over the edge. I came around his fingers and thumb, moaning into his mouth and feeling his come in between us. I could smell his seed, smell the sex, and feel his love all at the same time. "Griffin...you're the only man I ever want." I didn't think before I said the words out loud. Lost in the pleasure, I uttered the first thing that came to mind.

He watched me as I finished my orgasm, the arousal in his eyes replaced by a different emotion. His fingers kept working my pussy until I was finished, and then he stared at me like I was the most beautiful thing he'd ever seen. "I know, baby. And you know you're the only woman I'll ever want."

THE MATTRESS WAS comfortable and the master bedroom was nice, but it wasn't the same as Bones's place. It didn't have the same coziness, but I loved being in Tuscany no matter what. With him beside me every night, it was good enough.

I was dead asleep when a nightmare came to me. Knuckles was there, dragging me away from my family. He had Sapphire too, who was swollen with her pregnancy. She was in tears, and he had a gun pointed right at my temple.

My father was on his knees as a man held a rifle to his head. The horror on his face was because of what he was witnessing, not the gun at his head. The man pulled the trigger, and then my father's body fell to the ground.

"God!" I jolted upright in bed, gripping the sheets and tipping over as I lost my balance. Hot tears fell down my face, and I sobbed as the images remained glued in my vision. I tried to suck the air into my lungs, but there was never enough oxygen. "Oh my god…" My hand moved to my chest, and I felt my racing heartbeat.

Bones sat up and pulled me against him. "Just a dream, baby. A dream." He leaned down and pressed a kiss to my shoulder and then my neck. "It's alright."

"I'm scared…" I stared into the darkness, looking out the window to the fields that I couldn't see. There were stars in the sky because it was a clear night. I couldn't see anything else but the heavens above. We were alone in the middle of nowhere. No one was around.

"Hey." He forced me to my back so he could look down at me. "I'm here. You know what that means?"

I stared at him, my chest still rising and fall sporadically. The back of my neck was beaded with sweat, and it absorbed into the pillow. I could see his muscular outline and the hardness of his jaw. His blue gaze pierced me like blades.

"It means nothing will ever happen to you. Don't be scared."

Like his words were a lifeboat and I was about to drown, I moved into him and held on. I found comfort in his muscular chest, in the thickness of his arms. I moved my face into his neck and focused on the steady pulse as it vibrated under his skin.

He cradled me beside him, hiking my leg over his hip.

"I'd never let anything happen to you, baby. So when the nightmares come, tell them to leave. They have no power over you." He rested his face against the pillow beside mine, his confident gaze chasing the rest of my pain away. "I'm the only one who has any power over you."

My hand moved up his chest until it rested over his heartbeat. Steady and slow, it thudded with power. "I dreamt…that Knuckles took me and Sapphire. And…one of his men shot my father." I closed my eyes, reliving that painful moment that hurt me. I took a deep breath, reminding myself it wasn't real, and I opened my eyes again.

He stared at me with the same expression, his eyes unblinking. "I would never let anything happen to him either."

My eyes moved to his face, surprise in my heart. "You just said you wouldn't hurt him…"

"I know what I said. But I'd protect him as much as I would protect you—because I know what he means to you. That goes for the rest of your family too." His hand moved to my cheek, and his fingers slid through my hair. "You're everything to me, baby. And I never want my baby to be scared or sad. Your pain…" He rested his palm over my heart. "Is my pain."

BONES PULLED up to the winery in his truck.

I sat in the passenger seat, feeling resentful toward my family before I even opened the door. My father was blinded by hate, and so was everyone else. If only they understood how much this man loved me, they would be able to let go of the past and move on.

But the Barsettis were so damn stubborn that didn't seem possible.

Bones looked at me when I didn't hop out right away.

I was almost tempted to ask him to drive back to the house.

He killed the engine. "One day at a time." Like he

could read my mind, he addressed the sadness in my eyes.

"Yeah…"

Bones went to work, working in the warehouse where the bottles were placed in the boxes then dollied to the storage facility before they were placed on the truck for delivery. This man was undeniably rich, and now he was working for free—for someone else.

I went into the tasting room and hung up my paintings on the walls. The nails were already there from my previous works, so these were easy to hang. I arranged them based on color, grouping similar images together so the presentation was more aesthetically pleasing.

Mom came to my side. "They're lovely."

"Thanks."

"Which is your favorite?"

"I don't know…I don't really have one." My favorite painting I'd ever made was sitting in my apartment. Nothing else I ever painted compared to that work, probably because I'd never felt so emotional in all my life.

"Not a single one?" she asked, her arms across her chest.

"Well, my absolute favorite isn't on this wall…"

Mom nodded in understanding, her eyes still looking over the fifteen different pieces I'd put on display. "I wonder how long it'll take for you to sell them all. A week? The weather is nice, so we'll have a lot of business."

"A week seems a little unrealistic."

"You don't know how much people love these paintings. I didn't have to pitch them at all. Everyone enjoys their wine and cheese and gazes at them. They seem to feel something, something so strong they can't leave without that picture. You'll see." She turned back to the bar. "You want to help me out today?"

"Sure." Bones would be working all day, so I should give myself something to do. "Hand out wine all day and talk about it? Sounds like a walk in the park."

Mom smiled. "Just don't drink all of it."

"Well…we might have a problem there."

We'd just finished setting everything up when my father walked inside, wearing dark jeans and a long-sleeved black shirt. His muscular arms and shoulders stretched the fabric, and it was so nice to see him stand tall, looking healthy and unafraid. It was the perfect anti-dote to my nightmare, to see him alive and well. Overcome with emotion, I came around the bar and hugged him. I held on, my arms squeezing his torso as my face rested against his chest.

My father looked down at me, hesitating before he returned the embrace. "Everything alright, *tesoro*?"

I nodded. "I had a nightmare last night…"

He patted my back and gave me all the time I needed. "Your mother used to have bad nightmares too. It'll pass."

"I know…it's just nice to see you." I turned away, hiding my face so he wouldn't see the emotion in my eyes. I headed back to the bar and pulled out the bottles we would be serving that afternoon.

My father kept looking at me.

My mother watched him. "So, Griffin is working in the warehouse today?"

Father stopped staring when my mother addressed him. "Yeah. Hector called in sick anyway, so that worked out."

"Yeah, it did," Mom said noncommittally. "Vanessa and I will do the tastings together. Her paintings are on display, and I'm sure people will be mesmerized by them, as usual."

Father turned around and admired the paintings he hadn't noticed before. He walked up to them, examining with the same diligence Bones gave when he looked at my creations. Father moved his hands into his pockets and stared at them, devoting a lengthy time to just stand there when he had a business to run.

I knew I shouldn't care what anyone thought of my artwork, but my family's opinion mattered to me. Bones's opinion mattered to me too. Seeing my father study my work so closely filled my heart with a special kind of warmth.

He pointed to the one on the top left. "That's my favorite of this bunch." It was a painting of the city of Florence from the edge of the countryside. Erect and tall in comparison to the low hills, the city stood tall like a skyscraper. "I've seen this very view all my life, driving to town or the market…" He turned back around. "But I like them all."

"Thanks, Father." I smiled.

Father came back to Mama then kissed her on the cheek. "Free for lunch?"

"I'm always free for lunch. You're the one who usually isn't."

"Well, I'd like to set some time aside for you today." She smiled. "I'll think about it."

He kissed her on the cheek again before he walked out.

I'd always noticed my parents' affection since I was young. It was the kind of relationship I wanted to have with my husband someday. Little did they know, it was the exact relationship I had with the man I loved—right at that very moment.

———

THERE WERE a lot of guests that afternoon, all visiting from Florence to try some of the famous Barsetti wine. They ordered cheese to pair with the different varietals, and I enjoyed doing something with my time that wasn't so isolating. When I painted, I rarely interacted with anyone else. I spent all afternoon in silence, creating pieces based on thoughts, memories, and feelings. Most artists were solitary people, and I guessed I was that way too.

But I enjoyed mingling with the tourists and locals who stopped by.

And to my surprise, people really did love my paintings.

Couples talked about their favorites, people asked about the prices, and a few even bought one before they left.

Before lunchtime arrived, I'd made over ten thousand euros.

I couldn't believe it.

I walked over to a table with two young gentlemen who seemed to be brothers, based on the way they were causally insulting each other. I poured the wine and noticed they'd been drinking quicker than anyone else in the group. "So, which is your favorite?"

"The 2008 was great," the one on the right said.

"2014 was better." The one on the left was dressed in a white t-shirt with a gray blazer. He had light skin and an American accent, so it didn't seem like he was a local. Maybe they were visiting with family. He had an indifferent demeanor, like nothing was good enough for him. "We were just at the Burtolli Vineyards. Now that's excellent wine."

I couldn't care less what this jerk thought, but I didn't appreciate the casual way he insulted the hard work of my family. "Then maybe you should go back." I poured the wine a little too fast and purposely spilled it on the sleeve of his jacket.

"Hey." He dotted the stain away with a napkin. "Watch what you're doing."

"I was." I smiled then walked off, helping another table that actually had some manners. I spent the next twenty minutes mingling and asking where everyone was from. My mom did a great job doing the tastings because she was from America, like most of the tourists. So she had visited the places where they were from and gave people a sense of familiarity.

As the customers started to taper off for lunch, Mom left early to join my father for their date. I stayed behind and finished off the final bottles and cleaned the glasses. The two jerks from earlier were still there, and now they were staring at my paintings.

I ignored them, waiting until they finally left so I could never think about them again. I wiped off all the tables with a rag and then rinsed the glasses people had drunk from before placing them in the dishwasher. We bought all our cheeses from the local village, so everything was fresh and authentic.

"Three thousand euros?" the man in the gray blazer asked. "This looks terrible. Did a five-year-old make this?" His arms were crossed over his chest as he looked at the paintings like they were trash.

I refused to let his opinion bother me. He was just some entitled asshole.

"Yeah," his brother agreed. "Amateur and pathetic. They had much better artwork in Milan. You know, by real artists."

The man in the gray blazer squinted at my name in the corner. "Vanessa Barsetti...no wonder it sucks. It sucks just like their wine." He seemed to say it loudly on purpose—for my benefit. After they thoroughly destroyed my day, they walked out and thankfully left.

Now I was finally alone...

His last words lingering in my mind.

I shouldn't let it bother me, let it tear me down. He was just one asshole, and everyone else loved my work. I wouldn't have sold four paintings that afternoon if I didn't have any talent.

I kept trying to convince myself his words didn't matter, but the fact that I had to try to convince myself at all told me his words did bother me.

Made me doubt myself.

Hurt me.

I stood at the counter with my eyes averted, making an effort to keep my breathing regular. I felt the emotion creep up on me, and it filtered through my veins. My eyes started to well up, and I did my best to keep them back. My strength waned the longer I had to fight against my reaction, because it just made me feel weaker.

I felt pathetic for letting it bother me.

Heavy footsteps sounded against the cobblestone floor. "Baby, what's wrong?"

I looked up to see the stunning blue eyes that contained my whole world. Strong and powerful, he invigorated me with strength just by looking at me. The t-shirt he wore had been soaked with sweat around his neck and armpits because he'd been working hard in the warehouse. A line of sweat covered his brow. When he was hot and sweaty, he looked even sexier than usual.

I came around the bar and moved into his chest, feeling my lifeline right under my fingertips. He was my strength as well as my weakness. He was my rock, the crutch I leaned on when I needed it most.

His hand moved to the back of my neck, and he stared down at me, concern in his eyes.

I thought I heard footsteps again, and I feared that asshole was coming back to insult me once more. But then I realized it didn't matter if he were…because Bones would kill him. And I wouldn't stop it from happening.

"Baby, what is it?" His fingertips moved under my jaw, and he lifted my gaze.

"It's stupid…"

His eyes narrowed. "Nothing you say is stupid. Tell me."

"Well…there was this guy who came in today. He was an ass, said our wine wasn't very good. Then he stared at my paintings and said…not very nice things. Said I sucked…like my family's wine. I know I shouldn't let it bother me because his opinion doesn't matter…but it hurt."

His eyes softened. Instead of telling me to buck up like he normally would, he gave me sympathy. His fingertips moved across my cheek. "Your paintings represent your soul. If anyone insults them, it's like insulting your feelings, emotions, beliefs…it's not stupid that it hurt you."

I turned my face into his palm, treasuring the warmth and strength.

"But he's wrong, baby. He doesn't possess your creativity, your beauty. And if it doesn't exist inside him, then he can't spot it when he sees it. His opinion is invalid. Your artwork speaks to people. I don't know shit about art, but it's made me feel so many things. You painted me, all of me, down to my very soul. How many people could do that?"

I watched his gaze, seeing the sincerity in his pretty eyes.

"You have a gift, baby. Soon, you're going to have your own gallery. And one day, people are going to be auctioning off your work for millions. When you're dead and gone, generations into the past, people will treasure your work because it captured the beauty of your life. It'll make you immortal." He cupped both of my cheeks, turning my face up a little more to look at me. "Don't listen to him."

I gave a slight nod, feeling better.

He wiped away my tears with the pads of his thumbs. "No man deserves your tears—not even me."

My hands gripped his wrists, feeling the strength transfer from him to me. "Thank you…"

He moved his lips to my forehead and gave me a long kiss, his warm mouth resting there for a while. "You're the most amazing woman I've ever known. You shine like the sun. Don't ever let anyone take away your light. A real man should never tear down a woman, but lift her up."

"That's what you do for me."

He wrapped his arms around me and lifted me into the air, pulling me against his chest so we were face-to-face. "Yes, I do."

My arms wrapped around his neck, and I pressed my forehead to his as my legs wrapped around his waist. "I love you."

He closed his eyes as he held me, our heads pressed together. "I love you too, baby." He held me that way for a while, letting me cling to him for comfort. Minutes passed before he returned me to the ground. "I should get back to work. I've got a lot of stuff to do."

"They're really putting you to work, huh?"

"Yep. Who doesn't love free labor?"

I smiled at him. "Thanks for doing this…I know you have a million other things you should be doing."

"Yes." He rested his fingers against my chin and lifted my gaze. "But this is the only thing I want to be doing." He gave me a soft kiss on the lips before he turned away. He held his wide shoulders with perfect grace as he walked away, his strong physique possessing a strong posture.

I watched him go until he turned the corner.

Then I heard the sound of footsteps again. I turned toward the door to see who it was. I caught a glimpse of my father's long-sleeved black shirt before it disappeared in the crack of the partially open door. I wondered if he'd been watching that entire exchange. My father wouldn't eavesdrop on me because he respected me too much.

But when it came to Bones, everything was different.

FIVE

Conway

I came around to the passenger side and helped Muse out of the car. She was five months along, and now her belly was noticeable no matter what she wore. She'd wanted to get married when she was still slim in a gown, but that didn't seem possible anymore. She would show no matter what—but I didn't mind at all.

The doctor said our baby was healthy.

When he said those words at his office, my throat tightened.

My son or daughter would be here in four months, and as Muse got bigger and rounder, the truth became more and more real.

I was going to be a father.

I took her hand and guided her inside my childhood home, the three-story mansion where my parents still spent their time together. Lars greeted us by the door, and then we stepped inside.

"How are you, man?" I hugged Lars. "You look damn good for a hundred."

Lars smiled, his hands shaking a bit. "Thanks, Mr. Barsetti. The ladies always like an older man."

I chuckled and patted him on the back.

"Sapphire, you're looking beautiful," Lars said. "Nothing more beautiful than a glowing woman. I remember when Mrs. Barsetti was pregnant with Conway. She's never looked more radiant."

"She definitely didn't look more radiant with Vanessa, that's for sure," I teased.

My parents came down the stairs to greet us. My father came first, greeting Sapphire before even looking at me. "Sweetheart, you look nice." He hugged her and kissed her on the cheek. "My son has been taking care of you, right?"

"Waits on me hand and foot," Sapphire said.

It was the truth. I wanted to make sure she was relaxed and happy. The doctor said stress could contribute to a miscarriage, and the idea scared me so much that I'd been doing everything to make sure that didn't happen. Ironically, I didn't want to be a father when she became pregnant, but now that her belly was big, I felt like a father without a child.

My mother greeted her next. "So beautiful." She hugged her for a long time, squeezing her gently. "I can't wait to meet my grandbaby. I know they'll be so beautiful, with both of your features."

"I'm excited too," Sapphire said. "I can't wait to see if it's a boy or girl."

My parents stared at her, watching her rub her stomach.

I cleared my throat. "Uh, hi?"

"Oh, sorry." Mom tapped herself on the forehead. "We're excited to see you too, son." She hugged me.

I rolled my eyes. "It didn't seem like it."

"You know I love you." She squeezed me. "I'm just so excited about the baby. We're going to have a new Barsetti around here."

My father came next, the usual affection gone from his eyes. There was no reason for him to be upset with me, but something was obviously bothering him. He hugged me, but it wasn't long or deep. "How was the drive?"

"It was okay." I didn't ask what was really bothering him, knowing I should do it in private.

"Are you hungry, Sapphire?" Mom asked. "Lars made dinner."

"I'm always hungry," Sapphire said. "I used to have a small appetite, but now I can't seem to stop."

"Being pregnant is the best," Mom said with a laugh. "Let's go into the dining room."

I turned to follow them, but my father grabbed me by the arm. "I want to talk to you alone in my study."

We didn't have private conversations in the study unless some serious shit had hit the fan. "What is it?"

He nodded toward the stairs, refusing to share that

information with me while we were out in the open. We headed to the third floor and then stepped inside his study with the two leather couches, the paintings with buttons, and the endless supply of liquor. As per tradition, he poured two glasses of scotch.

My father had asked me to come down for a visit, but he never said why. I knew now he was about to tell me. "Enough with the anticipation."

My father held the glass between both of his hands but didn't give an answer. His head was bowed, slightly in defeat. "I wasn't going to tell you any of this because I thought I could handle the situation on my own. I figured the problem would be gone almost a month ago. But since it's not going anywhere, I can't keep it from you. You should know what's happening..."

I was actually scared, afraid of what my father would say. There was nothing he couldn't fix, so whatever this was, it was big. "Tell me."

"Alright." He set the glass down, not having taken a drink. "It's gonna be a big pill to swallow. It's about Vanessa."

My sister was the most annoying brat on the planet. She infuriated me as much as she demanded my respect. But I loved her so much, would do anything for her, so the second her name was mentioned, I was scared on a whole new level.

"Remember Bones? The man you saw at the Underground?"

Like I'd ever forget seeing my enemy's son. "Yes..."

"Vanessa is seeing him."

"Seeing him how…?" There was no way she was dating him. That was preposterous.

"Dating him," my father said. "Seriously dating him."

I heard every single word, but my body rejected the sentence. My spitfire sister was sleeping with the son of the man who'd damaged our lives? "Are you sure?" Vanessa was too smart to do something like that. She was too stubborn, like the rest of the Barsettis. "That just doesn't sound right."

He nodded. "I'm sure. She told me she loves him…"

My fingers slackened, and I almost dropped my glass. "What?"

He nodded again. "I knew she'd been seeing someone for a while, but she never introduced him to us. Your mom talked to her about it a few times and knew Vanessa was intensely in love with someone. I told Vanessa I wanted to meet him, reminded her that she's old enough to introduce me to a man she loves. And that's who she introduced me to…Bones."

I rubbed my temple. "You've gotta be fucking kidding me. That fucking asshole? What the hell is she thinking?"

He held up his hand to silence me. "It's shitty. I agree. I've talked to her about it a lot, met with him a lot."

"You came face-to-face with him?" I asked incredulously. "And he's still alive?"

My father smirked. "He's been trying to get my approval. I've seen him a few times for dinner and whatnot. He's assured me he means no harm to us. He genuinely loves Vanessa. And if I don't accept him, he won't come between us and Vanessa…he'll walk away."

This was the last thing I expected to hear. "You think he meant it?"

He nodded. "Seems like it. He's talked to me one-on-one. He's come into my home, handed me a loaded shotgun, and handcuffed himself to a chair to prove himself to me. Now he's helping out at the winery, trying to spend time with me so I can see who he is…"

I still couldn't wrap my mind around this. "This has been going on the entire time?"

"I thought I was going to get rid of him in a few days…but he's still here. He's like a damn cockroach that just won't die." He finally took a drink, immediately clenching his jaw once the booze was down his throat.

"Why haven't you ordered him to stop seeing her?" That sounded like the best solution. Bones said he would back off if my father didn't approve. So that was all he had to do.

"Because…" He stared into his glass as he swirled it, the stress written all over his face. No matter what obstacle he faced, he was always fearless. He kept calm under dire situations, and even when bullets were flying, he was in control. But now, the worry was in all his features. "Vanessa asked me to try to accept him. She asked for a real chance. Because she loves him and knows I love her enough that I don't want to hurt her. So…I guess I'm trying."

"His father killed my aunt," I snapped. "No, you don't have to try, Father."

He raised his hand again. "I understand how you feel. It's the way I've felt for the past six weeks. I've said some very unkind things to Vanessa that I shouldn't have said… because I resent her for putting us in this situation. I don't like him, and it's hard to imagine a time when I'll ever like him, ever trust him."

"Then end it," I said. "Or I'll kill him for you—for all of us."

"Not so simple," he said.

"Father, it is simple. Vanessa deserves someone better. Don't ever tell her I said this, but she's fucking incredible. Smart as hell and fierce like a soldier. She deserves a good man."

"I agree," he said with a sigh. "But he's the man she wants…unfortunately."

"She'll find someone else. Plenty of fish in the sea."

He set his glass down. "Their relationship is intense… strong. I can see it between them. It makes me hate him even more, that he won my daughter over so completely. But the worst part is…" He grabbed his glass again and took a deep drink, prolonging the inevitable. He licked his lips when he was finished and set down his glass. "I think he really loves her."

It was hard to believe a man like that could love someone. He came from a cruel father, and he was at the Underground for a reason. I didn't want a man of the shadows for my sister.

"I've seen them together." His eyes formed a haze as he thought of a memory. "I've seen the way he treats her when no one is watching, the way he lifts her up and makes her feel good about herself. The way he worships the ground she walks on. The way he takes my insults even though it makes him want to kill me. The way Uncle Cane punched him twice and he still didn't do anything. I don't think it's an act...I think it's real."

I couldn't picture this relationship. I couldn't picture my sister loving a man like that, and I certainly couldn't picture a man like that loving a Barsetti. It didn't seem possible. It went against nature. "Even if it is, you can still end it. She'll hate you for a while, but not forever."

"This is the thing about having children." He refilled his glass. "I should tell you this since you'll be a father soon. No matter how old they are...you want them to be happy. And despite my reservations and my hatred for him...which is very intense...I see the way he makes her happy. Because of that reason, I may accept him. I'll never like him. I'll never trust him. But...I think I should try to give Vanessa what she wants."

I couldn't believe my father actually said those words. Vanessa was his only daughter, and he was far more protective of her than he'd ever been of me.

"So, I think I'm going to try to get to know him better, to stop insulting him, and to see the man Vanessa has fallen in love with. Honestly, I've never really tried. I've only made him feel as unwelcome as possible. He's never pretended to be something that he's not, and he's very transparent about who he is…which makes me respect him. He also told me that I was hypocritical for not accepting him, considering your uncle and I aren't exactly the most noble people…and he's right."

My relationship with Sapphire wasn't exactly respectable. I paid for her virginity and practically kept her as a slave. I was afraid to tell my father the truth because of what he would think of me, but he said it would be hypocritical to judge him. Now, I treated Sapphire the way she deserved…but it hadn't always been that way. "But Vanessa deserves more."

"I agree." His eyes moved down. "But…this is what she wants."

My father was taking this exceptionally well, but I couldn't picture myself doing the same thing. I didn't trust Bones. I didn't want him anywhere near my sister or my fiancée. "I don't think I can be as calm about it."

"I felt the same way in the beginning. It's taken time to be this civil."

"Don't expect me to be civil."

He held his glass between his hands. "I figured you wouldn't be. Doesn't make a difference to me. Just don't hit him."

"Why?" There wasn't a good enough reason for me to keep my hands to myself.

"It won't solve anything. And every time he takes a hit without reacting, his power grows. He proves that he's the man he claims to be. Don't give him the opportunity to prove himself in any way. Your uncle almost broke his hand against his face. It's like a slab of concrete."

I remembered exactly how he looked, all muscle, tattoos, and a solid bone structure. He had a tight jaw, a stern expression, and shoulders so broad he looked like an ox. He was a large man, the kind that could break a man's skull with a single fist. His size was accompanied by handsome features, looks he must have inherited from his mother. He was the kind of man who could get laid instantly. I'd seen the way the waitress looked at him that night, like she was waiting for him to invite her back to his place once her shift was over. "Then what's the plan?"

"I'm going to try. But we need to be prepared if things go to shit."

I nodded in agreement. "What is the likelihood he would do something?"

He dragged his finger around the rim of his glass as he considered my question. "It's hard to say. He's already been seeing Vanessa for a while. He could have attacked us much sooner with the element of surprise. Doesn't make sense for him to go through all of this just to hurt us. A lot more time and effort than necessary. And like I said before…I think their relationship is real. So he may never do anything, but we should always be prepared for the off chance we're wrong. I always have a gun on me whenever he's around. You should do the same. Your mother has one too. I hate being armed in my own home, hate increasing security around the house and preparing for war when I've dedicated my life to peace…but I don't see any way around it."

I resented Vanessa for doing this to us, for bringing a criminal into our lives like this. She could have any other guy she wanted, but she had to pick the worst possible person. "What do you know about him? What does he do?"

"He's a hitman."

I remembered reading that in his file. He owned a business with a few men. Other than drinking too much and spending money on whores, there was nothing else interesting about him. He did his job then went home. "Anything else?"

"No. He's been honest about everything I've uncovered about him. But he did tell me his mother was a prostitute after his father died. She was killed by one of her clients when he was just a boy. He had a vendetta against us ever since…and dropped it after he fell in love with Vanessa. I don't see why he would tell me that unless it was the truth. Part of me believes him. Part of me thinks letting it go and accepting him would bring us all peace. But another part of me…will never stop hating him for what his father did to us." He bowed his head and turned silent, his finger still moving around the rim of the glass.

I would never look at the man as anything but an enemy. I would always have my guard up, even if she married him and five years had passed. I would never allow him around my wife and children without being present. He would never be welcome in this family. I might be stubborn like my father, but I didn't care. "I'll never stop hating him either."

———

I ARRIVED at the small villa after dinner. Father gave me the address, and I didn't feel intrusive slamming my fist against the solid wood of the door. Sapphire was at my parents' house, watching TV in the living room with a mug of hot cocoa in her hands. My parents adored her, thought the world of her. They never cared she modeled lingerie or came from humble beginnings. I loved her—and that was enough for them to love her too.

The door opened, and I came face-to-face with him. Bones.

When I'd seen him at the Underground, he'd been wearing some kind of disguise. But now he was exactly as I remembered from the pictures in his file, his gray t-shirt hugging his muscular frame and stretching across the shoulders. Ink was all over his arms, sleeves of tattoos with midnight-black coloring. He was my height, and his crystal blue eyes were the only thing about him that wasn't innately dark. With fair skin he must have inherited from his mother, he was distinctly different from the Barsettis.

He stared at me, his guard up just as high as mine. He knew exactly who I was, and now I knew he recognized me in the Underground. He didn't try to kill me that night—for unknown reasons.

"You want to talk to Vanessa now? Or would you like to punch me first?" He tilted his head slightly, regarding me with subtle hostility.

"Punch you?" I asked. "I usually stick a knife in the throat of my enemies." My father told me to keep my eyes peeled and my hands to myself, but when I was face-to-face with Bones, it was impossible to be diplomatic. He didn't deserve my sister.

"You wanna do that, then?" he asked, dead serious. "I'm sure I could handle it."

My father was right. He had a natural ability to turn threats into signs of power.

"My father told me not to kill you—yet."

He smiled. "That was nice of him. Can never tell how much he hates me."

"I'll be the messenger, then. He hates you a lot."

Vanessa ducked underneath his arm and squeezed past him in the doorway. "So glad you two are getting along…" She moved up to me, her arms crossed over her chest. "What are you doing here?"

"You know exactly why I'm here." My eyes flicked to Bones again.

"To kill him?" she asked incredulously. "When you brought Sapphire around, I became her best friend. It didn't matter whether she was a good person or not. You loved her, so I had to love her. I accepted her without an interrogation."

My eyes turned back to her. "Are you suggesting these

situations are the same? This man is a murderer, Vanessa. He kills people for cash. His family—"

She raised her hand. "I've had this exact conversation with Mom and Dad, like, fifty times. I'm not doing it again."

I looked at Bones, the hatred in my eyes. "Disappear." I wanted to speak to my sister alone, not have that gargoyle watch everything.

To my surprise, he shut the front door and walked away.

Vanessa stepped farther into the cool air in the front yard, approaching the truck parked in the gravel. "So, Father told you today?"

"A few hours ago." I slid my hands into my pockets and followed her. "I've gotta be honest. I'm pretty shocked."

When we were away from the house so we couldn't be overheard, she turned to me. "I know he's not ideal. But I never wanted to love him. It just happened. And now that it's happened…I never want to love anyone else."

My father wasn't kidding. Their relationship was intense.

"I know you're probably never going to like him, Con. That's fine. I'm not going to try to persuade you to change your mind. But I hope one day you'll have an open mind. Because of Sapphire's past, I was kidnapped by Knuckles. I've never been able to sleep well since that night. Bones makes me feel safe, makes me feel like nothing could ever hurt me. I've never held Sapphire accountable for that night or ever blamed her for what happened. I love her, as my sister and my friend. She's family as far as I'm concerned. And if I can do that, I don't see why you can't do this for me."

My sister had always been better with words than I was, and she'd made an astounding point. Because of Sapphire, Vanessa had been shot. Now she would carry a scar for the rest of her life. At the time, she'd acted so brave, but of course, it bothered her. Nightmares followed her every night. I didn't know what to say because she made such a fair argument.

She watched me as she waited for me to say something. "Don't say it's different because it's not. I would do anything for Sapphire because you love her. You know how I am, loud and opinionated. But the second it was clear that Sapphire was the only woman you wanted, I was supportive and loyal. I made her feel like family more than anyone else. I became her friend when she had no one else. She could have been a total bitch, and I still would have treated her the same way." She stared at me with her hard gaze. "I love this man with all my heart."

I took a deep breath when she confessed her feelings, hearing the sincerity ring like a bell.

"I don't want anyone else. I'll never want anyone else. Mama and Father are trying to accept him. I'd appreciate it if you would do the same. I don't expect it to happen overnight, and Griffin is very patient. But I've always been there for you when it mattered—and I've been there for Sapphire. When Knuckles offered to make the exchange of me for Sapphire, I told you not to do it. I was willing to die for the woman you love. You owe me this, Con. Big-time."

I clenched my jaw, having no argument against that at all. My sister had paid her dues, had been unflinchingly loyal to me. I would give this to her in a heartbeat under any other circumstance. "I don't trust him, Vanessa. I don't trust him not to kill our family."

"Trust is something earned, not given. I would never ask you to trust someone you didn't know, Con. You never have to trust him if you don't want to. You don't even have to like him. I'm just asking for acceptance right now. The rest of that stuff will come later…when you're ready."

I'd never anticipated my love for Sapphire would come back and bite me in the ass. "Can you really be with a man your entire family hates? I just talked to Father, and he despises him more than anyone else on the planet. You're smarter than this, Vanessa. Find a better man and don't put your family through this."

"I tried to forget about him, Con. I broke up with him when he told me he loved me. I dated someone else. I did everything…it didn't work. I knew I loved him so much I was willing to do anything to make it work. As slim as the odds are, I want you guys to learn to like and accept him. He's willing to be a punching bag to make it happen. If it doesn't work, at least I tried. I had to try before I gave up." She took a deep breath, her chest rising. "But I don't want to give up. The way I love him…is the way you love Sapphire. Just keep that in mind when you talk to him."

"But how do you know he's the right man to love? How do you know this isn't a plot to hurt all of us?"

Her eyes watered slightly, like the question offended her. "Because he would die for me, Con. Would a man die for me if he didn't love me with all his heart?"

I kept my hands in my pockets and stared at her, feeling the chilly air surround me and enter my lungs. I saw a different side to my sister, a vulnerable side she never let me see. Her beating heart was on her sleeve, visible for the whole world. All of her cards were on the table, and even though she had a shitty hand, she wasn't ashamed.

"Please try," she whispered. "For me."

SIX

Bones

Vanessa was the first thing I looked at every morning.

I opened my eyes, and she was there, her beautiful skin bright in the morning light. Her olive skin contrasted against the white sheets. Her thick eyelashes were luscious and feminine. I studied her for a while before I turned her over and made myself welcome between her legs.

Evening used to be my favorite time of day. Now it was the morning.

Because this was how every morning was.

My arms pinned her knees in place, and I moved between her legs, greeted by her tightness and wetness. I woke her up slowly, watching her eyes flutter open as the pleasure circulated in her veins. She enjoyed sex the most when she was half asleep, when all her sensations were heightened. Her hands eventually pressed against my chest, and she looked at me with sleepy eyes.

Beautiful.

I loved the way she looked at me, with nothing but love, lust, and devotion. She gave herself to me despite all the odds against us. She told her brother I was the man she loved, told her father she wanted to be with me forever. She stood up for me in spite of the overwhelming obstacles in our way.

I breathed against her mouth and listened to her moan for me, her nails digging in a little harder as I made love to her slowly. Her moans became louder, her nails became sharper, and then she came with a moan that shook the house.

I came next, filling her perfect slit with all my come. It was how I started every morning, making love to my woman before I hauled shit all day. Her uncle and father refused to acknowledge my existence unless they were insulting me. It was tough work, especially when I could be doing anything else. But these mornings made it worth it, this time when we didn't say a single word to each other. We just clung to one another, made love, and then started our day afterward.

I loved every morning.

We both showered so we wouldn't smell like sex and then headed to the winery. We didn't talk about her brother's visit last night, probably because nothing about it was surprising. Conway hated me like everyone else.

Not exactly news.

We drove in silence, Vanessa sipping her coffee in the passenger seat with her sunglasses on her nose. She wore a red sundress today, low-cut in the front with her hair curled and pulled to the side. She wore a small sun hat, fitting in with the Tuscan countryside perfectly. This place was in her blood.

I knew the men who came to the wine tasting would stare at her all afternoon.

But they couldn't have her—she was mine.

We arrived at the winery then hopped out of the truck. She was heading into a different building, so I walked her to the cobblestone patio and then peered down at her, tempted to kiss her.

She gave me a slight smile, knowing exactly what I was thinking. "See you later."

I hated staring at her like this, staring at her like I couldn't have her. No one was around, but I didn't want to cross the line and piss off her father for the afternoon. He was looking for any reason to get rid of me, so I couldn't risk putting him in a bad mood.

She moved her hand to my forearm and gave me a gentle squeeze.

"Yeah. See you later." I turned and let her hand slide away from my arm. I walked into the warehouse where the wine was filtered and processed. Wine was bottled and then the bottles placed in boxes. My job was to move those heavy boxes and prepare them for shipments. It was hard labor, but I was committed to outperforming any other worker they had.

They would never acknowledge it. But at least I would know.

I got to work and immediately worked up a

PENELOPE SKY

sweat, the moisture darkening my neckline, underneath my arms, and along my back. Sweat formed on my forehead, but I kept working through the morning, knowing my woman was across the way, refilling wine for her customers. She looked beautiful in that red dress with her dark skin. Her mascara made her eyelashes thicker, and her eyeliner brought out the natural color of her eyes. I smiled as I thought about her, the most beautiful woman I'd ever seen.

And she was mine.

Crow stepped inside the warehouse, dressed in all black. A pistol sat on his hip. He scanned the warehouse before he looked at me.

I knew he didn't wear a gun at work on a regular basis. His toy was just for me.

How flattering.

I kept working, assuming he was looking for something else besides me.

Crow walked up to me, his muscular shoulders stretching his t-shirt. His black wedding ring sat on his left hand, the metal reflecting the sunlight that came through the windows. His dark gaze was on me, telling me had something to say.

I wiped my hands on my jeans then straightened, meeting his gaze with my own. I never knew what Crow was going to throw my way. He was unpredictable, keeping his thoughts deep behind his eyes. He had a great poker face.

Crow moved his hands to his hips, his hand dangerously close to his gun.

I was always afraid of the moment I was dreading, the moment when he would tell me to leave Vanessa and disappear. It was my worst nightmare. The longer I was with Vanessa, the harder I fell. She was such an incredible woman, so strong and so compassionate. She put up with her family's hatred of me, but she somehow remained loyal to both of us at the same time. If she wasn't such a good artist, she should have been a diplomat.

Crow seemed unsure what he wanted to say, because he kept staring at me like he was indecisive.

I wanted to start the conversation, but I was too afraid to come off sarcastic or cold.

Crow finally found the right words. "Come with me." He turned around and left the warehouse.

I watched him go, wondering where he wanted to take me. I followed a second later, trailing behind him across the dirt to the first building that housed the restaurant and entryway. Once we turned down the hallway, I realized we were going to his office.

Which meant he wanted to talk.

Shit.

This could be it.

The moment he took away the greatest thing that had ever happened to me.

We stepped inside his office and shut the door, and Crow sat on one of the couches in front of his desk. He had a bottle of scotch on the coffee table along with two glasses. He rested his elbows on his knees and stared at the spot where he wanted me to sit.

I lowered myself across from him, my hands coming together. It was the first time I'd ever been nervous around him. Any other time, I was fearless, refusing to let any man intimidate me. But now, I was scared. Scared that this man had so much power over me. I told him I would leave his daughter if he asked—and I had to keep my word.

I just hoped he didn't ask me to do it.

How could I wake up every morning without her beside me? How could I find another woman to please me and not think about Vanessa? How could I live a life without her light, her love? I'd never been dependent on anyone for anything, but now I'd become dependent on Vanessa for my happiness.

She was my whole fucking world.

I helped myself to the bottle and poured two glasses.

Crow didn't take his. He kept staring at me, looking at me like he wasn't sure what to say again.

Since this silence could go on forever, I started talking. "Don't take her away from me. I'm not the kind of man who begs, not even for his life. But I'll beg for her. I wasn't a good man before we met, but she's made me into one. She's my world. I'm not ashamed to say it. I'm not ashamed to admit that I need her."

Her father was just as stoic as before, looking at me like I hadn't said anything at all.

I preferred his insults to this silence. I couldn't read him—at all.

He lowered his head and looked at his hands for a moment. "I don't like you. I'll never like you. I don't trust you, especially around my family. But…I'm going to try to accept you. I think you really love my daughter, and I know she loves you. So…let's have a drink."

I repeated every single word inside my head, treasuring those words like they were gold. He insulted me at first, but then he said what I wanted to hear. He gave me the chance I'd been working for. He gave me the opportunity to keep Vanessa. I knew that was hard for him to do, that his paranoia was warning him this was a terrible idea, but he was putting himself at risk—for his daughter.

"I've never really tried with you. I've been too busy insulting you. My brother punched you. The list goes on. So…tell me something about yourself. Something that won't make me want to kill you." He grabbed his glass and brought it to his lips for a drink.

I didn't know what changed his mind—and so abruptly. Vanessa and I hadn't done anything differently. I'd kept my head down and tried to be as nonthreatening as possible, and Vanessa was still fighting for me. Nothing seemed to have changed. "I wasn't expecting this."

"I said I'm trying to accept you," he said coldly. "Never said I already had." He drank from his glass again. "So, tell me something about yourself."

There weren't many topics we could touch. My childhood was off-limits, and my adult life was even worse.

"I'm not that interesting. My life only became worth discussing when I met Vanessa."

"Then tell me something about her."

I grabbed the glass and held it between my fingertips, thinking about all the things I couldn't say. Like the way her mouth parted when she came, the way her voice deepened to such a powerful tone when she exploded around my dick, and the way she whispered her love when I was buried deep inside her. "When she paints… she has this cute look on her face. Like, she's doubting herself through every step of the process. She stops and thinks about the next place she's gonna rest her brush before she finally commits, because she knows every move she makes is permanent. She's not just artistic, but pragmatic."

"She was always secretive about her artwork. She never allowed us to watch her process. I'm surprised she allows you to do it." It was the first time Crow had said something back to me, a reply that wasn't hostile. It was just a rebuttal, the second part of the dialogue.

"She doesn't. I watch her when she thinks I'm not looking."

Crow drank from his glass, his eyes on me.

"In her art room, there's a large window that stretches from the floor to the ceiling. When I stand in the doorway, I can see her reflection. That's how I see her face when she's painting, the way she deliberates before placing the brush in the paint."

He set the glass down then wiped his lips with the back of his forearm.

"She's a very easygoing person, but when it comes to her artwork, she's very serious. She cares about it deeply, but that's not surprising considering how talented she is. I don't know anything about art, but I know her art is… there are no words." When we talked about Vanessa, our conversation didn't seem so tense and forced. "What was she like as a child?"

"Selfish, bratty, a little know-it-all," her father said bluntly. "But adventurous, beautiful, and strong. They said fathers push their sons harder than their daughters because they expect more out of them. That wasn't true in her case. I spent far more time pushing Vanessa to be a strong and capable woman like her mother. Fortunately, Conway didn't seem to care too much. He was ready to be a man by the time he was sixteen, ambitious, serious, independent…" He looked at his glass as he remembered her childhood. "I taught her how to fight, how to handle a gun, how to think critically …which explains how she escaped Knuckles. I told her to never wait around for a man to save her, not even me. I taught her to save herself."

"I see a lot of her in you…and vice versa."

"Not sure if that's a compliment."

I'd hated the Barsettis for so long, but spending time with them had taught me to respect them. They were honest, honorable, and compassionate. If Crow didn't love his daughter so much, he wouldn't be sitting with me right now. "It is. It's the reason I fell in love with her in the first place. She has bigger balls than most men I've met. She stood up to me when men twice her size would have shit their pants. She didn't hesitate to try to kill me, unlike most women. She's told me off more times than I can count… I never knew that was the kind of woman I was looking for. Headstrong, confident, fierce…I respect her. She's the first woman who didn't just earn my respect, but commanded it. I see where she gets it."

He picked up the glass, lightly tapping the side with his finger. "When I met my wife, she was the same way. Outnumbered and outgunned, she stood no chance at all. But that didn't stop her from fighting. She put me in my place so many times. I respected the way she never stopped fighting. And I wished that my sister had been the same way…had fought harder and longer." His eyes lifted up to meet my gaze, pain in his look. "I was close with my sister the way Conway and Vanessa are close. Conway looks after her even when I've never asked him to. They argue, but he loves her with all his heart. When I told him you were in the picture, he said his sister was amazing and deserved better, deserved the best. I wish I could tell Vanessa what he said, but he forbade me."

"She already knows."

He set his glass down, the condensation making a ring on the wood. "It's been over thirty years, but I've never gotten over it. When my parents were gone, my sister turned into a daughter to me. As the oldest son, I became responsible for my two siblings. I was there when your father pulled the trigger. I watched the bullet enter her skull and spray blood everywhere. Her eyes had been on me at the time, and when she was dead, they just glossed over… It's the kind of shit you never forget." He grabbed his glass and took another deep drink. "Your father told me to bring twenty million, and he would make the trade —her life for the cash. I showed up and did exactly as he asked. He took the money and killed her anyway." He looked at me, his gaze full of accusation, like I'd been present that very night.

We were supposed to keep the conversation light, but we'd somehow returned to our roots. "I'm sorry." My apology meant nothing in this situation. His sister's death wasn't my fault, but as my father's son, I felt obligated to right the wrong.

"Sorry for what?"

"My father wasn't a good man. He did something unforgivable to your family. I can't apologize for what he did because I wasn't alive when this happened. But I am sorry for wanting to follow in his footsteps, for ever wanting to hurt your family in the first place. You're good people…you deserve better."

"Don't kiss my ass."

"I'm not." I set my glass down and rested my elbows on my knees. "I think you're blindly stubborn and need to let go of the past. I think your brother is a hotheaded idiot, and you're the arrogant but pragmatic one. I'm not afraid to be real with you. But I do acknowledge the wrong my family committed against you. I never should have wanted vengeance. I shouldn't have been so stubborn and narrow-minded. My father provoked your family in the first place. He's the perpetrator, and you're the victim. I see a lot of Vanessa in her mother, and knowing what my father did to Pearl is starting to make me a little sick…" I took a long drink of my scotch and returned the glass to the table. "Now that I love a woman with all my heart, I constantly want to protect her. The idea of something like that happening to her… I don't even want to talk about it."

Crow kept a straight face even though discussing this probably killed him inside. "My wife is a survivor, not a victim. That's not how I see her. That's not how she sees herself. Would never want her to view herself in any other way."

"When are you going to talk to Vanessa?"

He shrugged. "I'm not sure. My wife has made peace with the past. She's been happy for a long time. To stir up those memories will just bring her down. It'll be hard for her to talk about it, especially with her daughter."

"I can imagine…"

Crow opened the bottle again and refilled the glasses. "Do you watch sports?"

"Occasionally. You?"

"Never."

"Then what do you do?"

"I work then go home to my wife," he said. "What else would I do?"

"Sounds kinda boring," I teased.

"You think so?" he questioned. "Then what's your day like?"

"I work in the morning and then…" My voice trailed away when I realized my life was the same as his. I immediately went to Vanessa, watching TV on the couch or making dinner together in the kitchen. My whole life revolved around her. There were no more parties or late evenings on the town. Everything else had been sacrificed to accommodate for the diamond in my life.

Crow gave a slight smile before he drank from his glass. "Look who's boring now."

"Yeah…guess so."

He set his glass down. "I've talked to my wife about this situation many times. It's all we talk about now. I mentioned the similarities between our relationships and asked her about it…asked if she would change anything. Her answer was no…that there wasn't a better man for her out there. She didn't have any regrets, any moments when she wondered if she'd made the wrong decision. She wonders if you're right for Vanessa…and we just can't see it right now."

"I am right for her." I fought for her every single day, and I wasn't going to downplay my confidence. "I'm the only person man enough for her. I make her stronger, and she makes me the strongest man on the planet. I don't come in a pretty package, but you don't want me to come in a pretty package. I'm like a guard dog that scares everything off. You can sleep well knowing I'm taking care of her."

He shook his head slightly. "I don't feel that way at all."

He'd insulted me a lot, but none of his taunts ever pierced me as deeply as that one.

"I'm constantly worried about her. My dying wish is to know my two children are safe. With Vanessa, I don't feel that way. I'm afraid I've given her the foolish belief that she's invincible. She thinks she can handle you, and now she's put so much confidence in her strength that it's become her weakness. She's blinded by lust, and it's clouded her judgment. I want to know my daughter is taken care of by a great man, not just someone who can provide for her and take care of her...but be good for her. To love her the way I love her, to care for her as the small woman that she is. That's what I want...and I don't feel that way about you."

I could barely get the question out. "Why? You told her you want her to be with a powerful man, someone who can take care of her. I fit that bill perfectly. Nothing can get past me."

"But you're also a target. One of these days, something is going to go wrong. Someone is going to want revenge. An attack will arrive, and you'll never see it coming. You won't be able to protect her."

"I'd die before I let anything happen to her."

"And in this case, you may both die. The only way to ensure that doesn't happen is to get off the radar. Live a quiet life with honest work. Keep your head down. Practice a life of peace and quiet. That is the only way to make sure she's safe."

It seemed like he was asking me to quit my job, the only job I'd ever known. It paid my bills and gave me purpose. It gave me an outlet to release my rage. Without it, I wouldn't know my identity anymore.

"When my wife told me she was pregnant, that's when I left that life. I told my brother I was leaving the arms business and focusing on my wine. Stepping away from crime and corruption was the only way to give my family the life they deserved. Karma came back for us, almost ripped us apart, and then Cane left his business and joined mine. Ever since then, it's been nothing but quiet. It was hard in the beginning, but I don't have any regrets. When I found out my son had been going to the Underground, I made him promise to stop and stay away. I don't want to get mixed up in that lifestyle ever again. You're the gateway to that. If you really want to be accepted into this family, you're going to have to choose. If you really want to prove yourself to me, you'll have to make that sacrifice. No way around it."

Now the option was laid before me. I had to give up my line of work for the woman I loved. "I'm just the messenger, the neutral third-party. I get paid to kill someone. Nothing personal. My victims only care about the person who ordered the hit, not who pulled the trigger."

"Grief does crazy things to people. You expect them to be that logical? If someone killed my wife, you think I would stop at the person who ordered the hit? No. I would go after every single person involved. If you really believe you're immune, then you're a lot dumber than I anticipated."

"I would be able to handle anything that came our way."

He sighed. "Your arrogance scares me more than your stupidity."

"You don't feel confident that you could protect your wife?" I asked incredulously.

"I do. Because I've removed myself from the possibility of threat. I don't give people a reason to kill me. Therefore, it doesn't happen. You, on the other hand, are making an enormous list of possible attackers. Every night she stays with you, I grow more uncomfortable by the second. When I was your age, I was arrogant too. I didn't care whether I lived or died because I had nothing in my life so valuable. When I met my wife, nothing changed in the beginning. But as I fell in love with her, I realized she was the most valuable thing on the planet. Guns and bulletproof vests wouldn't protect her. Only disappearing would. I made a sacrifice that was hard to make, but she was worth it. So tell me, is Vanessa worth the sacrifice? Because if she is, I'll take you a lot more seriously."

Now he'd put me on the spot, asked me a question point-blank. He wasn't going to give me much time to think about it. I never wanted to leave my business because it gave me a sense of purpose, the way art gave Vanessa a sense of purpose. Every person needed something to live for. All I'd ever known was killing. It paid well, and it gave me a serious adrenaline rush.

He kept staring at me, not dropping his gaze until I gave an answer. "I asked you a question."

"And it's a pretty heavy question, Crow. I need time to think about it seriously before I spit out an answer. I don't want to say something I regret, especially when I can't take it back."

"I don't see what there's to think about," he said coldly. "You would either walk away from that life to protect her, or you wouldn't. Which is it?"

"Vanessa would never expect me to quit working for her."

"No. But I do. You want my daughter? Prove it. Prove to me that you'll take care of her."

My temper was rising, but I did my best to keep it sheathed. "I need money to take care of her."

"You have more money than you'll ever need. You can retire—we both know it."

Looked like he dug into me pretty extensively if he knew my finances.

"You do it for your own personal reasons. You get off on putting a bullet in someone's head."

"Like you're any different," I countered. "You were just like me when you were my age. I've never been unclear about the man that I am, but you continue to sugarcoat the man you used to be."

"I'm not sugarcoating it. I just don't think it's relevant."

"And I don't think it's relevant for me because I'm not the same guy anymore. Vanessa changed me—for good."

"Then quit," he snapped. "Walk away. My daughter deserves a man who will protect her, not bring danger to her front door."

I brought my hands together, my knuckles starting to ache from the anger in my veins. "I kill bad men, Crow. I don't kill random men who don't deserve to die. I've killed more sex traffickers than any country's law enforcement. I've killed men who've beaten their wives or tortured their prisoners. I'm not a hero by any means because I'm doing it for the money, but it's not like I murder innocent people."

"Spin it however you want, it doesn't make a difference. Once your feet hit the puddle, you leave tracks everywhere you go. One day, you'll take the wrong mission and wind up dead because of it. I don't want Vanessa to be caught up in the middle of that."

I understood his request, but that didn't make me want to cooperate. "I run the business with my boys. They're family to me. We met on the streets, and since we didn't have anyone else in our lives, we became brothers. Asking me to leave is asking me to turn my back on them."

"I don't give a shit. If they're really your family, they'll understand."

Maybe. But they wouldn't be happy about it.

"So?" he pressed. "What's it going to be?"

"I can't give you an answer right now." I wasn't going

to give one until I was absolutely certain I could commit to it.

He gave me a disappointed look. "Maybe Vanessa was wrong about you."

I didn't know what that meant, but I didn't like it.

"She said you would give it up if she asked."

"I haven't given my answer yet."

"Because you don't want to give her what she wants," he said quietly. "What I want."

"This is unfair. No one asked this of you."

"Because no one had to," he snapped. "I stepped up. I did the right thing for my wife and son. I shouldn't even have to ask you this. Neither should she."

"She's never asked me."

"My wife never asked me. A man never makes his wife ask for anything. He lives his whole life for her, even if she doesn't see the sacrifices that he makes."

"Fine," I countered. "If I walk away, are you guaranteeing your acceptance?" I wasn't going to leave my business without that reassurance. It was time for him to put his money where his mouth was.

He drank from his glass, silent.

"I asked you a question."

The bottom of his glass hit the table. "Don't push me."

"If you want me to give up one of the most important things in my life, I want collateral. You give me your word that I'm accepted into this family, and I'll resign tomorrow. You get what you want, and I get what I want."

He stared at me, refusing to give me an answer.

"What's it going to be? Is Vanessa worth the sacrifice or not?" I was turning his words against him, putting him on the spot and forcing him to make the hardest decision of his life. It was disrespectful and risky on my part, but how could I earn the confidence of a man if I didn't stand up to him? I had to show him I wasn't afraid to stand up to anyone.

"You're the one proving yourself to me, asshole. I've already proven my love for my daughter a million times over. The fact that I'm sitting here, sharing my prized scotch with a man I despise, is more than enough proof. If you want my daughter, you have to earn it. You may be rich and powerful, but that's not enough. Nothing is enough when we're talking about Vanessa Barsetti, the most amazing young woman on this planet. I want to see more than you've given me, more loyalty, more sacrifice."

"I've sacrificed everything for her," I said between clenched teeth.

"No. Not everything. Not yet."

JUST WHEN I'D made progress with her father, that progress was destroyed.

He seemed to want to accept me, but he also wanted to sabotage me. He was looking for any reason to get rid of me, to find the smoking gun that could banish me from his life forever. He wanted to prove to his daughter that he was making a genuine effort, but he also wanted to prove that he was right.

I wasn't good enough for her.

It was a stupid point to prove because it was obvious. I never said I was good enough for her. No man was. I just knew I loved her more than anyone else, would die for her in a heartbeat. That was good enough for me.

I worked in the warehouse for the rest of the day, moving heavy boxes everywhere and making sure none of the precious merchandise fell to the floor and shattered. The spring had brought heat into the land, and by the end of the afternoon, my t-shirt was soaked.

I stepped outside so the fresh air could blow over my skin and lick away the sweat on my arms and neck. The view of the vineyards was as beautiful as the paintings Vanessa made. Her art showed me what she loved about this land, and I recognized the view she'd stared at so many times. I felt like I was connected to her, having stood in a place she stood before.

Footsteps sounded to my left, and I turned to see Mrs. Barsetti walk toward me. She had a cold bottle of water in her hand, and she extended it to me.

I gave her a nod in gratitude and took it, ignoring the pistol that sat on the hip of her jeans. She'd been carrying since Crow started to carry his. He probably made her do it, wanting her to be protected even if he wasn't around.

But she obviously wasn't scared of me. Her stupid gun wouldn't have any effect on me if she pulled the trigger.

Mrs. Barsetti possessed youthful beauty that still made

her a very pretty woman. She was slender with an hour-glass figure, having a body that didn't seem like it had given birth to two children, let alone a son who towered over her. She kept her skin safe from the sun, so her face and neck were still unlined and smooth. She had blue eyes as I did, something neither of her children had inherited.

I twisted off the cap and took a long drink. I consumed half the contents before I tightened the cap again. "Thanks."

"Of course. There's water in the break room. You've proven yourself to be an ox, so please help yourself when you need something."

I worked myself hard, constantly trying to prove to the Barsetti family that I was built like a machine. I could go on forever, even if I got a migraine from dehydration. I could work ten times as hard as any other employee they had. My strength and endurance were unquestionable.

I waited for her to walk away, assuming she didn't want anything to do with me. She seemed to be more understanding than her husband, but she was also more restrained. She basically told me she was only partici-pating because she knew her daughter loved me.

Mrs. Barsetti brought her hands together as she stared at me. "My husband told me you guys had a long talk…"

"Yes. And it ended the same way all the others do."

"I know you're frustrated. You do a decent job hiding it."

"It doesn't matter how frustrated I am. I'm not going anywhere."

"I know," she said quietly. "I admire you for putting up with all of us. I know my husband and brother-in-law aren't the easiest to get along with. They've both been very stubborn. It's just how they are. And when it comes to Vanessa…they get a little crazy."

"I get crazy when it comes to her too."

"Yes, I know," she said with a chuckle. "Why else would you be here every day?" She stepped onto the dirt path that moved down the hill toward the vineyards. "Walk with me."

I was timid whenever it came to this woman. "I'm not sure your husband would like that. I'm trying to get him to like me…not give him another excuse to hate me."

She patted her gun on her hip. "Don't underestimate me. I'm an incredible shot."

"That's not what I'm worried about."

"Don't worry, he knows what I'm doing." She kept walking. "And he knows I can handle myself."

I followed her, and we moved into the rows of grapes. She explained the system to me, how the fruit was harvested before it was processed in the warehouse. She picked grapes right off the vine and popped them into her mouth, not caring if there was a bit of dust on them.

I didn't care how wine was made, but it was nice to talk about something else besides my worthiness of being accepted by the Barsetti family.

"That's a quick tour," she said as she kept walking. "I learned all of this when I started helping Crow at the winery. For the longest time, he wanted me to stay home and get fat, but I insisted I needed to be involved in something."

"He wants me to stay home and get fat too."

"I know," she said. "But that's a very different situation." She stopped at one spot in the row and faced the rest of the fields as they stretched into a valley. "We've been growing the vineyards for the past thirty years. Now we have locations everywhere, and there's more work than can possibly be handled. Cane managed the wineries in other places, but the work never seems to end. We always hoped Conway would take over, but obviously, he has no interest in it. Then we were hoping Vanessa would want to take over...but she seems more interested in artwork."

"It's what she's meant to do." I wouldn't pity her parents for not having someone to pass their livelihood on to. Vanessa was so painfully talented that it would be a disgrace if she spent her time doing anything else. "I know she's going to be huge someday, have paintings hanging in museums."

Mrs. Barsetti stared at me, the corner of her mouth rising in a smile. "You really believe in her."

"Absolutely. Anytime I look at her pieces, I feel everything she wants me to feel. That's impressive because I'm not an emotional man. But she makes me feel love, beauty, peace, heartbreak...with just paint and a canvas. I'm sorry she's not interested in taking over the family business, but her destiny lies elsewhere."

"I know. Her father and I always dreamed both of our

children would want the business so we could see them all the time. But of course, they have their own lives."

"Vanessa wants to be close to you, whether she's working at the winery or not."

"Yes, I noticed that." She smiled. "She was so eager to get out of here when she first moved out, but now she seems to miss her roots."

"She does. She wants to settle down here and start a family. She'd live right next door to you if she could."

She smiled wider. "You have no idea how happy that makes me…"

"You should hear the way she talks about you and Crow. She shows you nothing but respect and affection. Anytime I've ever tried to undermine you, she's told me off for it." I kept up my transparency, wanting them to trust me to always be truthful.

"I appreciate your honesty…"

"But I see why she feels that way. It's a beautiful place, and I see the way all the Barsettis love her. She has a family, a community of people who adore her. Sometimes it baffles me that she's still fighting for me even though her entire family hates me, especially when she could have another man in a heartbeat." Vanessa could have any man she wanted. All she had to do was flash her pretty smile, and they would fall at her feet.

"Vanessa had never had an intense relationship with a man before you came along. Whenever she told me about the men she was seeing, it was with forced enthusiasm. There was always something about them she didn't like, even if they checked out on paper. But when she met you…I've never seen her be so passionate about anyone. Honestly, you make me uneasy, but I trust my daughter… trust that she knows what she's doing. She's a smart woman and doesn't put up with bullshit. Therefore, you must not be bullshit."

"I'm not."

She started to walk away. "You know how Crow used to be at your age. You know how our relationship used to be. It wasn't a fairy tale. He wasn't Prince Charming. But I fell so deeply in love with him that I didn't have a choice but to spend the rest of my life with him. I've never had any regrets about the decision I made. I accepted him for exactly who he was, all the darkness and all the light. How can I tell my daughter to leave you when I didn't leave my husband?"

I appreciated her bluntness. "I couldn't agree more."

"But I still feel a warning in my heart when I'm around you, like this could be a big mistake. You've wanted to kill me…" She turned around and looked me in the eye, like she was searching for my vengeance. "I killed your father…and you've wanted to kill me ever since." She was challenging me, luring me out into the fields where we could speak openly about the divide between us.

I used to want to stab her the way she stabbed my father. This woman took everything away from me. My inheritance was given to someone else. My mother had to become a whore to support us. We were punished for a crime we never committed.

"Will you ever be able to look past that?" she whispered. "Look past what I did?"

Her beauty masked her coldness. She was a powerful woman just like Vanessa, the kind who didn't show fear even if she was terrified. Vanessa got her strength from her father as well as her mother. I could see it. "I already have."

"Because I'm not sorry about what I did. Your father did terrible things to me. He didn't just rape me but beat me for the hell of it. He let his friends take turns with me then injected me with drugs to wake me up when I passed out from the pain."

I flinched at the announcement, feeling pity for this woman even though I hardly knew her.

"He got what was coming to him, and I would do it again in a heartbeat. I loved watching him die on the floor, his blood spilling everywhere. Ever since he died, I've slept like a baby."

I held her stare, surprised I didn't feel any rage at her words. Knowing the same thing happened to my mother had changed my perspective on women. I didn't want them to be used for their bodies, treated like livestock rather than humans. I couldn't rape Vanessa because of that reason, because it was innately wrong.

I didn't want to be that kind of man.

"You did the right thing," I said quietly. "You deserved justice. You deserved peace."

She tilted her head slightly, regarding me with focused eyes.

"I've always been resentful of the life that was taken from me, the wealth and security. My mother would still be alive right now, and I wouldn't have had to live on the streets. Losing my father wasn't what killed me inside…it was losing my mother. And that never would have happened if you hadn't killed him. I've been jealous of the life Vanessa has, having two loving parents and a mansion, along with a family business. But I've overcome my jealousy and pain…because your daughter completes me." She kept the shadows out of my heart and sheathed my anger with her love. "I've learned to accept what I lost…because I have her." I hadn't said those words to Vanessa, that I'd become so pathetically dependent on her for my happiness. But she knew…I was certain she knew.

Her mother was quiet for a long time, examining me with a guarded gaze. She crossed her arms over her chest, her gaze tilted up. "I want to believe you…so I'm going to try. I'm going to try to look past my own issues and accept you as a new man. It's not fair for me to punish you for what your father did. You deserve the opportunity to be seen as your own man. But knowing you've wanted to hurt my family…will make me suspicious of you for a long time."

"Understandable." That was more than I could possibly ask for.

"My husband believes you really love my daughter."

It was the greatest compliment I'd ever received from the Barsettis, and it balanced out all the insults that had been thrown my way. The only reason I was there was because Vanessa was the only woman I ever wanted. I wanted her so damn much I suffered their judgments constantly. "I do."

"And I want to believe you do too."

I GOT inside the shower as soon as we got home, wanting to rinse off the endless line of sweat that had trickled down my body all day. The warm water rinsed my body, stripping away the endless conversations with her parents.

I'd talked to them more than I talked to Vanessa.

I'd never been on a job interview, but getting along with her parents seemed to be the longest job interview in the history of time.

I stood under the water a few extra minutes, enjoying the peace and quiet the falling water provided. My relationship with her parents seemed to be improving, but their suspicion of me hadn't faded. At any moment, they could slam the door in my face and tell me to leave.

And I would lose Vanessa.

I hated allowing someone to have this kind of power over me. It would be easier if I just killed them all so nothing would stand in my way. I could finally have Vanessa all to myself. If I didn't love her so much, I would be seriously tempted.

But she would never forgive me.

I stepped out of the shower and dried my hair with the towel. I was the kind of man who did the least amount of work possible when it came to my appearance. I only shaved once a week, and right now, my chin was getting thick with hair.

I walked into the bedroom naked and stopped when I saw the exquisite sight in front of me.

Vanessa was in black lingerie, something she must have picked up without me knowing. It was a bodysuit made out of thin lace, and it had a fastening between her legs I could open and fuck her through without taking the whole garment off. She was on her knees in the center of the bed, resting back on her ankles. A piece of black rope was on the bed in front of her.

Jesus Christ.

I slowly stepped toward the bed, my cock coming to life in a nanosecond. I stared at the black rope, the surface smooth so it wouldn't leave marks on her delicate skin. I fisted it and tested the strength, loving the way it hardly stretched.

It had my approval.

Her hair was curled and around her shoulders, and her heavy makeup made her look like she was ready for a photo shoot. Her eye shadow was black, bringing out the intense green color of her eyes.

"Had a change of heart?" I glanced at the rope.

"I think you earned it." She spoke in a quiet and husky voice, her shoulders back and her nipples visible through the thin fabric of her lingerie. She grabbed the rope and wrapped it around both of her wrists, showing me the way the dark rope looked against her olive skin.

I was witnessing my own fantasy, watching this beautiful woman ask me to tie her up and fuck her relentlessly. I'd tried tying her up on several occasions, but she never went for it. "I haven't earned anything. You don't owe me anything." I grabbed the rope and pulled it from her wrists. "I want to do this if you want to do this." There were other kinky things I wanted to do, but I never pressured her because it seemed unlikely that she would go for them. It was the kind of stuff I usually had to pay for. Besides, having her in my bed satisfied me every night. There was nothing I was missing.

"I do. Now tie me up and fuck me." She extended her wrists again, her eyes challenging me with their hard gaze.

A shiver ran all the way down my spine. Her voice didn't catch in her throat, and her strength never wavered. She trusted me so deeply that she wasn't scared of anything. She was giving me the power to do whatever I wanted, and she was confident I would take her somewhere she wouldn't want to leave.

I tossed the rope back on the bed and grabbed her by the arm. I yanked on her hard, forcing her to fall forward onto the bed. I made her turn over, so she was looking up at me, her face upside down from mine.

I quickly tied the rope around her wrists, securing her hands together with the perfect amount of rope in the center for me to grab on to. I gripped it and pushed it down, forcing her arms over the edge of the bed and toward the floor.

My face hovered over hers, my eyes close to her mouth. I watched her chest rise and fall quickly, the tension burning in her blood. She probably expected me to keep it vanilla, to playfully restrain her so I could fuck her quickly.

Not my style.

I pushed her hands down farther, taking all the power away from her. In this position, she couldn't move at all. She tried to fight me, but at this angle, there was nothing she could do. She pressed her thighs tighter together, fighting both fear and arousal at the same time.

My mouth brushed against her cheek as I moved to her neck. I breathed into her ear before my lips finally touched the pulse in her neck. I kissed the skin, dragging my tongue across the softness, and then I moved to the top of her chest. The lace barely covered the valley between her tits, so I dragged my tongue down the cleavage line. I tasted her, feasted on her.

She took a deep breath, her body slightly arching to get more of my mouth.

I smiled as I kissed her, not surprised by her enthusiasm.

I made my way back down and held my mouth over hers, our faces opposite of one another. I teased her, dragging my lips over hers without actually kissing her. I felt her hands attempt to rise, but I held her wrists in place with a single arm.

I liked to torture her, to remind her who was in control.

Me. I was always in control.

I finally pressed my mouth against hers, bringing her bottom lip between mine as I sucked it. Whether she was upside down or not, the kiss was packed with explosive chemistry. I could barely touch her lips without losing control. My mouth moved a little faster, and I breathed a little harder. My tongue came next, and she greeted me with hers.

My hand moved down her body, right in between her gorgeous tits. I squeezed each one as I kept kissing her, touching my woman and worshiping her perfection. My mouth worked harder, and soon we were panting together, the fire burning in our veins.

She tried to lift her hands again.

I kept them pinned to the bed. "Don't. Move."

She sucked my top lip into her mouth. "I want to touch you…" She moaned in between my lips, filling my lungs with her desire.

"It's my time to touch you." I kept kissing her as my hand moved over her mound and in between her legs. I unfastened the opening, and when her pussy was exposed, my fingers took a dip. I slid two fingers inside her and worked her clit with my thumb, kissing her at the same time.

"Griffin…" Her arms moved up again.

"Move one more time, and I'll spank your ass."

That only made her moan into my mouth harder. She rocked her hips against my hand, making love to my fingers the way they were making love to her. Her kiss turned intense, and she was reaching for more of me.

I felt her pussy tighten around my fingers and her lips quiver against mine. I knew what was about to happen, but I refused to let her slip away. I pulled my fingers back and stopped the kiss, leaving her breathless and frustrated.

"Griffin." She pleaded with me with her eyes, begging me to keep going.

"You'll come when I say so."

She groaned in protest, and she used all her strength to raise her arms toward me.

This time, I let her do it, since I was going to enforce my punishment. I let her arms move up as her fingers reached for my hair. But instead of letting them hit their mark, I pushed them against her stomach and untied the rope.

Once her hands were free, she reached for me again, desperate to finally get her hands on me so she could enjoy me.

I grabbed her by the arms and forced her into a new position, her face against the mattress and her ass in the air. I pulled both of her arms back and tied her wrists together, being harsh on purpose because she'd disobeyed me.

And then I smacked her ass—hard.

"God…" Her body shifted forward from the force of my hit.

Her cheek was already red. "What did I say?"

She breathed deeply through the pain, moaning slightly.

"I told you not to move. What did you do?"

She didn't answer.

I spanked her again.

She moaned and jerked forward. "I moved…"

I gripped the rope between her two hands and pushed on her lower back, making her bend a little deeper. Then I directed my pulsing dick inside her, pushed through her wetness, and hit her deep and hard.

She moaned again but didn't move her arms since she was stuck in place.

I gripped both of her elbows and pounded into her forcefully, slamming into her pussy without a hint of gentleness. I usually made love to her because she asked me to, but now, all I wanted to do was fuck her. I loved my woman, but that didn't mean I didn't want to fuck her the way a man fucked a whore.

My hand moved to the back of her neck, and I gripped her as I thrust deep inside her, my balls swinging back and forth because I was moving with impressive speed. The longer I fucked her, the more I was greeted with her wetness. I stared at her tight little asshole as I kept her wrists pinned to the small of her back.

I could do this all night.

A real man should always fuck his woman like this,

make her feel how turned on he was. I knew she could feel how thick my dick was, feel how immensely hard it was just for her. I'd fucked a lot of women in my lifetime, doing kinky shit that was down and dirty, but none of those fantasies compared to this one.

Fucking someone I loved was so much better.

It made me appreciate her even more, the way she gave herself to me with complete trust. She was being treated like an animal, but because I was the one thrusting inside her, she enjoyed it. The rope was so tight around her wrists that she couldn't move, but she moaned through my thrusts anyway.

Such incredible pussy.

Her fingers tried to reach for my hand, but they were constricted too tightly in the rope. She moaned with my thrusts then gasped for air when I fucked her even more viciously. Her face was smashed into the sheets as my hand pushed her farther into the bed, but she never asked me to stop.

I leaned forward over her, my ass tight from clenching so hard. This was exactly how I wanted to claim my woman, tied up and defenseless. I could enjoy her however I wanted because I'd earned her. She gave herself to me freely, knowing I was putting up with bull-shit every single day just to keep her.

I earned this ass.

Her moans were muffled by the sheets, but her plea-sure was undeniable. Her pussy tightened around me, coating me with mounds of sexy cream. She covered me to the hilt, making the white liquid build up around the base of my dick and behind my crown. Her moans echoed inside the bedroom and passed through the walls, filling up every inch of the house.

She slowly wound down, catching her breath as her wrists fought the rope that bound them together.

I slowed my movements before I shoved myself deep inside her, coming with a loud moan. "Damn…" That moment when I dumped my seed inside her made me feel invincible. I had this beautiful woman with her legs spread, taking my cock with enthusiasm, and she loved feeling her pussy stuffed with my essence. She loved me despite my flaws, loved me despite her family's hatred.

I'd earned a damn good woman.

I wanted to keep coming inside her, to keep making her mine over and over again. I didn't untie the rope or let her face rise from the mattress. I kept her pinned in place as my cock softened. I pulled myself out and watched my own come drip to her entrance. I stared at it, my cock hardening again in pride. Nothing turned me on more than watching myself claim my territory. This woman was all mine.

And I was all hers.

SEVEN

Vanessa

When the alarm went off in the morning, I opened my eyes to see Bones staring at me.

He watched me, his blue eyes focused with their usual intensity. It was obvious he'd been watching me for a while because he was wide awake. He'd probably been waiting for me to wake up so we could do his favorite part of our morning routine.

I was still in the lingerie I wore last night, my crotch unfastened because he fucked me until we both went to sleep. I could still feel his come inside me, could feel the wet spots where it dripped everywhere. Laundry was a daily thing for us. If not, the entire place would smell like sex all the time.

He welcomed himself in between my legs, his muscular arms pinning behind my knees. Without saying a word, he pushed his crown inside me, moving through the come he deposited the night before.

My hand flew to his chest, and I gasped when I felt the pain. "I'm sore…"

He paused before he continued to slide in, this time moving slower. "I'll be gentle." He inched until his length was deep inside me. He hovered over me, watching me like he'd been waiting for this very moment for hours.

"You fucked me so hard last night…"

He kissed the corner of my mouth before he planted a soft kiss on my lips. "Don't wait for an apology. You aren't getting one." He slowly moved inside me, being the gentlest he'd ever been. His thrusts were soft, giving my body time to get used to the immense intrusion.

"I know."

He folded me underneath him and kept his face close to mine, taking me gently like a man taking a woman's virginity. He made love to me slowly, using the time to feel me and appreciate me. His lips moved with mine, matching the same pace as his thrusts. He sucked my bottom lip then gave me his tongue, making love to my mouth with his masculine intensity.

I loved waking up this way every morning. It was always the same routine, where we opened our eyes as soon as the sun rose, then came together for this kind of lovemaking. It never lasted very long because we both had things to do. But this moment in time, this pause, was what I looked forward to the most.

I wanted these moments every day for the rest of my life.

I knew he did too, even if he never pledged his commitment to me. He never told me he wanted to marry me, but I knew I was the only woman he ever wanted. We hadn't talked about having a family, but I needed to have children. He would give them to me if I asked. "You always make me come so good…" I could feel it approaching, feel the tightness in my stomach before the big explosion.

"Because I'm a man." He spoke against my mouth, his beard coarse against my soft skin. "That's what men do for their women."

"But you don't do this for all women…" My fingers moved up the back of his hair, and I watched the love in his eyes grow. "You only do it for me." He always made sure I was pleased before he released. My pleasure always came first, and I'd been with men who never cared about that. I'd had nights when I touched myself after a guy had left because he couldn't get me off. I'd never had that problem with Bones. He fucked me so much, made me come so much, that I was sore and spent most of the time.

He brushed his nose against mine, the love in his eyes. "Only you."

———

I TAPPED my knuckles against the slightly open doorway. "Can I come in?"

My father was sitting at his desk in a black t-shirt and jeans. His tanned skin looked darker than usual when he was inside and away from the natural rays of the sun. With strong hands, muscular arms, and the black wedding ring on his left hand, he still had the traces of a man in his youth. He'd aged well because he took care of himself. Sometimes people assumed my parents were very young when they had me, but that wasn't the case at all. They were older than I am now when they started their family. "Always."

I approached his desk, watching the way his features softened when he looked at me. That look was never there when Bones was with me. It was reserved for just the two of us, along with my mom. He was a much different man from when Bones was around. He could be himself when it was just us. The man I knew was affectionate, loving, and attentive. He wasn't the cruel man he turned into when Bones stepped into the room. "How are you?"

"Good. I just got a large order from one of our vendors. I didn't think we'd be able to fulfill it, but your ox of a boyfriend has been dominating that warehouse…so we have extra wine that's ready to ship out."

Bones was always sweaty by the end of the day. His clothes were soaked, and his muscles were thick with blood. Despite his exhaustion, I thought he looked sexy. I'd hopped into the shower with him a few times and happily got on my knees to suck him off. "He's working very hard to impress you."

"As much as it benefits me, I don't care about that. Productivity and efficiency aren't qualities I look for in my daughter's boyfriend." His eyes weren't aggressive like they usually were, so I knew he wasn't in a bad mood.

"But I think he's proven how dedicated he is. You can't disagree with that."

After a long pause, he gave a slight nod. "No, I suppose not."

Bones had told me that my father had a drink with him, tried to have a normal conversation with him. My mother did the same. It wasn't a huge step, but coming from my stubborn parents, it was a big deal. Before, all they did was tell him off. But now they were actually trying…even if they were struggling in the process. "That's why I'm here, actually. I wanted to thank you. I know how hard this is for you…for Mama too. But you're really putting in the effort and trying to get to know him…and it means a lot to me."

Father's eyes darted away, like he couldn't handle the words I'd just said to him. He looked out the window instead, his left hand tightening into a fist. He didn't seem angry, but my words obviously struck a chord with him.

I waited for a reply, but the longer the silence continued, the less likely I believed one was coming.

"I believe he loves you. But other than that, I fail to see the qualities you find so desirable. I never want you to forget your own worth, Vanessa. Not only are you smart, beautiful, and talented, but you come from a strong family. You could have any man you want. Don't ever forget that."

"I'm not settling, if that's what you think."

"I'm not sure what I think." He tapped his knuckles lightly against the table. "It's hard for me to understand your relationship, especially when it seems so deep. But I remind myself that your mother loves me with all her heart…and I've never understood why."

My father was the greatest man I'd ever known. Silent and strong, he showed his softer qualities only to those who deserved them. "I do."

His eyes shifted back to me, slightly soft.

"I don't think it matters who you used to be before Mama came around. All I've ever seen is two happy parents who would do anything for each other. I see the way you love her every day, the way you look after her when she's not watching. I see the way you fall more in love with her as you age. Bones reminds me of you in that regard. He may not have been the best man when we met, but he's come a long way. He loves me very much… the way you love Mama."

My father kept staring at me, speechless for one of the first times in his life.

I knew the conversation was over and my point had been made. A seed had been planted, and now I just needed to let it grow. I walked out and entered the hallway. When I reached the end, I came across Sapphire. "Hey, what are you doing here?"

She hugged me, turning her stomach slightly because

it was starting to get in the way. "Conway is helping your mom with a few things. We've kinda made this trip into a family vacation. He's finished his new line of lingerie, so he has some free time."

Knowing my brother designed sex clothes for women was a little awkward, but I never teased him for it. He was talented at what he did, and I was mature enough to accept it. My parents never blinked an eye over his choice of profession. "I'm sure it'll be great."

"He's going in a new direction this time." Her hand moved across her stomach. "A whole maternity section…"

Now it was really getting awkward. "Let's have lunch and talk about the baby."

"The baby?" she asked. "I think we have something bigger to talk about besides the baby…" She grinned at me before we headed to the restaurant.

I knew she was referring to Bones.

We grabbed a seat on the terrace, away from the other tables that had guests. I had an iced tea and she had water, and after we ordered our entrees, the bread was served.

Sapphire kept staring at me, a knowing grin on her face. "So…you wanna start talking? Or do you want me to start asking questions?"

"What did Conway tell you?"

"Everything your father shared with him. That this relationship has been going for a long time…" She gave me an accusatory look. "I was surprised by that part."

"And I'm sure you understand why I had to keep it a secret…"

Her gaze softened. "Yes, I do. Conway has been pretty upset about it, even after you guys talked."

"My brother is just as protective of me as my father." I stirred my drink with my straw. "And more stubborn, on top of that."

"I know," she said with a chuckle. "I've heard all the reasons why they hate Bones and don't trust him. But there's something else I've heard too…that they all think this guy really loves you."

At least they could see the truth of that. "Because he does."

"And I've also heard he's hot."

My jaw nearly dropped. "Who told you that?"

"No one said those exact words…but everyone has said he's got great looks," she said with a chuckle. "Even Conway said it. So, if Conway, your father, and your mother all mentioned it…then he must be pretty damn fine."

I dragged my hands down my face, thinking about the way he'd made love to me that morning. "You have no idea…"

"The sex is incredible?"

"Again, you have no idea…"

She tried to hide her smirk, like she was keeping a comment to herself.

"But it's more than that. I love him. I understand why my family hates him. I don't judge them for being so hostile about it. But we need to let go of the past and move on. He's not a threat to anyone, and he just wants to be accepted. I know in time, they'll even start to like him. They just have to keep an open mind."

"The fact that he's still around tells me they're keeping an open mind. If Conway weren't, he would have shot him by now."

"I know…"

"I think they're worried he might flip and change his mind, that we were all in danger."

"He would never hurt anyone. But maybe they'll believe that in time…"

She dipped her bread in oil and balsamic before she placed it in her mouth. "Honestly, it's hypocritical for Conway not to give Bones a real chance. I shouldn't tell you this…but he's not the most noble man in the world."

I raised an eyebrow, not sure what Sapphire meant by that.

"But I love him that way. I love everything about him, our entire story. I wouldn't change any of it for any reason. And from what I can tell, your father and uncle weren't much different when they were young. So…it's a pattern with the Barsettis."

It was hard to imagine my brother doing anything remotely wrong, considering how high-strung he was. "What are you talking about? And leave the gross stuff out of it." Sapphire was my friend, and if she were seeing someone else, I'd probably want to know all the details. But since this was my brother, the man who lit my dolls on fire when we were kids, I didn't want to know anything about his personal life that wasn't relevant.

"Long story short, I left his modeling company and tried to take off on my own. I was grabbed by traffickers and sold at the Underground, a place where men bid on enslaved women. Conway was there, and when he saw me, he bought me for a hundred million dollars so no one else could have me."

My jaw dropped. "He has that kind of money?"

"Apparently."

"And what was my brother doing at the Underground in the first place?" I refused to believe my brother would participate in the slave trade so openly.

"He and Carter run a business. Families pay them to rescue their daughters from the Underground. They pay for the women and then deliver them back to the families. He was there buying someone else when he saw me."

"Oh…that sounds pretty noble."

"Well…when he took me back to the house, he said he owned me. He said he could do whatever he wanted with me because he paid so much for me…including sleeping with me. I was a virgin, so that made him want me more. For the first few months of our relationship, that's how it was between us. Master and slave."

I covered my open mouth. "Seriously?"

She nodded. "I was never his girlfriend. I only told you guys I was so I would have some leverage over him. I said if he didn't treat me right, I would tell his family the truth, that he was keeping me as a slave."

"Oh. My. God."

"Yeah…"

"And you just fell in love?" I asked incredulously. "How do you fall in love with someone like that?"

She narrowed her eyes at me, like she couldn't tell if I was being serious.

That's when I realized what I'd just said. "I guess that's a hypocritical thing for me to say."

"A little," she said. "And it just happened. Conway started to show me the good side to him, and the more I saw it, the more I wanted it. We became close, became friends as well as lovers, and I never wanted it to end. I fell in love with him. When I told him, he said he didn't feel the same way."

"That's why you went to New York…"

"Yeah. Until he came after me. The rest is history. My point is, it wasn't a fairy tale. Conway's behavior was unacceptable by most standards. But that's how it happened…and I wouldn't change anything."

"Does my father know any of this?"

She nodded. "Conway told him everything."

My heart started to slam painfully in my chest. It pounded like a steel drum. "And he was just fine with it?"

"Sounds that way."

"Let me get this straight…" My hands were starting to shake because I was so angry. "Conway forces you to sleep with him because he paid for you, and my father is just fine with that? Because Conway was the man and you were the woman? That's fucking bullshit. Sexist bullshit."

"He never forced me," she corrected. "It's not like I didn't want to be with him."

"It doesn't matter," I snapped. "He wasn't a gentleman. He didn't take you out to dinner like a normal person. He just went for what he wanted."

"I guess…"

I threw my napkin on the table. "I understand that raising a son is different than raising a daughter, but my parents never treated us differently. They raised us to be exactly the same. It's wrong that Conway isn't held accountable for his actions, that my parents encourage your relationship, but Bones is put on trial."

"You're their only daughter, Vanessa."

"Whatever. It's wrong."

"Conway and I fell in love…so I guess that's why it's okay."

"And Bones and I haven't?" I asked. "It's a double standard."

"But you were the prisoner, Vanessa. Conway wasn't. It's different."

"Different, but not right." I sat back in my chair, feeling the pulse in my neck throb from the rage. "It's not right at all."

Sapphire stared at me with a look of sympathy. "Maybe I shouldn't have told you…"

"No, I'm glad you did. You made a good point. Barsettis are all the same. I'm no different. The men in my family are dark and powerful, and that's why I want a man just like that. Makes perfect sense to me."

She kept staring at me, her gentle eyes regarding me with concern. "If he's really the man you want, don't give up on him. Even if I had a family that told me Conway was no good for me, I wouldn't have walked away. I know he's the man I'm supposed to be with."

Bones was the man I was supposed to be with. "I'm very close with my family, so I always dreamed of having a husband who could be another member of my family. But now I realize my vision of my family isn't really accurate...they aren't who they say they are. They ignore their own crimes and judge Bones for his. It's not right."

"They'll come around," she said. "Just be a little more patient."

I didn't think I could be patient any longer.

BONES DROVE the truck back to the house, and I looked out the window of the passenger seat. I wasn't really in the moment because I was thinking about my conversation with Sapphire. Things seemed to be going well with my father, so that was why I didn't confront him about it.

I didn't want to provoke him.

Bones glanced at me every few minutes, taking his eyes off the road to look at my scowl. "I'm listening... whenever you're ready."

"What makes you think I have something to say?"

"I can tell when you're pissed, baby. You're practically seething."

My man knew me so well. He could read my mood like a thermometer could detect a change in heat. "I went to my father's office this morning and thanked him for trying so hard. I know it's difficult for him, but he's really making an effort. I wanted him to know how much I appreciated it."

"Why would that make you upset?"

"It didn't," I said. "But when I spoke to Sapphire later…that made me upset."

Bones drove with one hand on the wheel, his large size taking up his entire seat. He shaved that morning because his scruff was getting too thick. He seemed to do it on the days he wanted to bury his face between my legs. His coarse beard aggravated my inner thighs sometimes, so it was easier to do it when his face was cleanly shaven.

Whenever he stepped out of the shower with a clean chin, I knew what was coming.

"And what did Sapphire say?" Bones pulled off the road to the dirt pathway that led to the house. He parked the truck on the side and then hopped out, his weight shifting the truck the second he was out of the seat.

I shut my door then came around, reaching his side. "She told me about her relationship with my brother… which wasn't what it seemed. Basically, most of it was a lie. She was never his girlfriend…just his prisoner."

We entered the house, and Bones immediately took off his shirt once we were inside. "His prisoner, huh?"

"Basically. He paid a lot of money for her at the Underground so he was entitled to her virginity…and her freedom. He never meant for them to be anything more, but it just happened. He slowly began to change until he fell in love with her the way she fell in love with him."

"Are you really surprised?" He stepped into the kitchen and pulled out a bottle of scotch. "I told you the men in your family aren't saints. They're definitely sinners." He poured himself a glass but didn't offer me one. "And I say that in a nonjudgmental way." He smiled with his eyes before he took a drink.

Bones had been right all along. All the men in my family weren't what they seemed. They had tainted pasts, memories they weren't proud of. My brother's actions were excused because he loved Sapphire now. But why didn't that exception apply to me?

"Does your father know about this?" He pushed the glass across the counter toward me.

I stopped on the other side of the counter, looking at the glass but not taking it. "Yes."

Bones didn't seem surprised. He gripped the edge of the counter with both hands, his muscled frame hard from working long hours. His arms were a little thicker from lifting all day, and his thighs bulged a little more. "Your father doesn't care what Conway did. And that upsets you."

I nodded. "Since Conway is a man, it's perfectly fine. But with me…it's unforgivable. It's a double standard, and it pisses me off. I would have confronted him about it, but since our last conversation ended so well, I didn't want to make him angry. He seems to be leaning toward accepting you, and I don't want to screw that up." I grabbed the glass and took a drink, letting the burn blaze a trail down my throat and into my gut. It wasn't smooth the way wine was, with a refreshing taste of citrus and oak. It was just liquor, stripped down to its basic form. I pushed the glass back toward him.

Bones stared at me for a long time, more interested in my expression than the booze sitting in front of him. He cocked his head slightly, his intense gaze piercing. The man never smiled, and he had a special way of looking at me that made me feel so small. He was doing it now, staring at me like he could see right through me. "You're right, it is a double standard. But double standards exist for a reason. You're held to a higher level because you deserve better. I'm not happy about this situation either, but your father is right to be upset. I wouldn't have understood his thoughts six months ago, but now that I love a woman, I get it. You're the queen of my heart, and if some man treated you the way I treated you…" He turned his gaze away, his jaw clenching in anger. "I'd kill him. We fell in love, but that doesn't justify the way I treated you. Your father only wants the best for you. This situation is frustrating, but you can't get mad at him for that. You're very lucky you have a father who cares so much. Not every person is so fortunate."

My anger slowly faded away, and I stared at this man with a new set of eyes. Not once did he try to turn me against my family so he could keep me. He always put my self-interests first, knowing how much my father meant to me. He really loved me, and I hoped my parents would understand that someday. He sided with my father even when no one could hear him do it. He was pragmatic even when it didn't serve his best interests. "That's sweet of you to say."

"I'm not trying to be sweet. Just honest. I want your parents to accept me, but I understand why they may not be able to do it. And if that's the case, I'll walk away. I want to keep you, but I can't be treated like shit every day for the rest of my life. I need to be in an environment where I'm accepted for the man I am, not criticized every other minute. And you deserve to be with a man your family can welcome with open arms. Hopefully, that's how this ends…when we both get what we want."

"That is how it's going to end," I whispered. "My parents have made it this far. This wouldn't have happened if they weren't really trying. And if they keep trying, they'll finally see you the way I do. I know they will."

He grabbed the glass and finished it off. "Hope so."

"I know so." I told my parents how much this man meant to me, and I wouldn't feel this way about anyone else. Bones didn't treat me right in the beginning, but I quickly forgave him for it and fell in love with him… because of his darkness. I liked that he was rough around the edges, dangerous at all times, and so intense it made the air difficult to breathe. I loved his power and strength, the way he owned a room the second he walked into it. My father was a terrifying man, but Bones didn't hesitate when he faced him. He was a fearless man, so powerful that even bullets couldn't slow him down.

Instead of pouring another drink, he grabbed the bottle and dragged it toward him. "Get naked. I want to pour this scotch on your tits and suck it off your nipples. I want to drench your pussy and devour every last drop. The two things I love most…booze and my baby. I want to enjoy them both."

As if our serious conversation didn't just happen, Bones turned his thoughts to the one thing he loved above all else—sex. He wanted it all the time, several times a day. And even when we were finished, it seemed like he needed more.

This man always needed more—more of me.

AT THE END of the workday, Bones and I prepared to leave. We didn't talk much during the day. We didn't even see each other. He didn't take breaks, getting as much work done as possible so he could prove himself.

Even though he'd already proven how strong he was.

My father stepped out of the main building and caught my attention. "*Tesoro.*"

I stopped and turned around, trying not to be angry about what Sapphire told me. Even if I confronted my father about it, he would just repeat himself. He loved me in a different way than he loved Conway, so his expectations were different. "Yeah?"

He glanced at Bones, who stayed by the truck. He always looked at him suspiciously, like Bones would pull a stunt at the most random time. My father's gun sat on his hip, a loaded pistol.

I hated seeing my entire family arm themselves just because of the man I loved.

"Could you come by the house? Your mother and I want to talk to you."

"Uh, sure." I didn't know why they wouldn't just do it here. That meant it was something serious. My thoughts turned to Bones, wondering if they'd decided they couldn't accept him into their lives. "But if you're going to tell me you don't approve of Griffin—"

"That's not what this is about."

"Oh...okay. Should he stay at the house?"

"He can come. But I want him to wait outside."

"Father, you're scaring me."

He gave me a tight expression. "It won't be a pleasant conversation, *tesoro*. But I promise everything will be alright." He turned around and walked away.

I moved back to Bones.

He must have heard every word because he didn't ask. He opened the passenger door for me then got behind the wheel. He left the winery and pulled onto the road.

"I'm nervous…"

He stared straight ahead.

"Do you know what this is about?"

"I have a hunch."

"What?" I asked.

He was quiet for a long time, dismissing me by staring straight ahead. "Not my place to say. But I don't mind waiting outside until you're finished."

I didn't know what my parents wanted to tell me, but I was a little scared. If it didn't have something to do with Bones, then I didn't know what else they wanted to discuss.

Bones arrived at the house, and my parents were already there. He killed the engine and rolled the window down. "I'll be here when you get back."

"I don't understand why you can't come inside."

"It's a family matter. I don't mind waiting for you here, baby." He pulled me into his arms and gave me a tight squeeze before he released me. He gave me a kiss on the forehead before he pushed my door open.

I gave him one final look before I left and walked into the house. My parents were in the dining room, so I sat down and looked at the fresh coffee and pastries Lars had set out. I could feel the tension in the room, the approaching misery that was about to descend on us all. They didn't say hello when I walked inside. They weren't angry, but something was bothering them.

I stared at them. "You guys are freaking me out."

My father rested his hand on my mother's back, right between her shoulder blades. "It's time for the three of us to have a conversation. It won't be easy. But when we're finished, we never have to speak of it again. We can move on."

The realization began to hit me. I knew exactly what they wanted to talk about. I took a breath, unsure if I was prepared for the gravity of the situation.

My mom looked down for a while, like she was bracing herself for the words she was about to share with me. "The only reason why we're telling you this is because it has to do with Griffin...how our lives are so intertwined."

I was right.

"I don't want to get into the specifics of it because they really don't matter..." My mom lifted her gaze to meet mine. "I've been very happy for a long time, and I don't associate myself with my past. I've been nothing but grateful for the life I've lived, and I wouldn't change the past, not to sacrifice the present.

I wasn't ready for this. I wasn't ready to listen to my mother's pain.

"When I was your age, a little older than you are now, I was kidnapped and placed in the trafficking business. A cruel man bought me from the Underground. What happened after that doesn't matter, but that man was Griffin's father."

I wanted to force a reaction, but I couldn't. I already knew this, and listening to her say it made me feel dead inside. My mother hadn't deserved that. No woman did. I felt my father stare at me, watching every reaction that I made. "I'm so sorry, Mama..." I could hardly speak without my voice cracking. I felt the tears long before they arrived.

"Don't be sorry," she said gently. "It was a long time ago. Your father took me to punish Griffin's father because of what he did to your aunt. He kept me as a prisoner for a while, but we fell in love quickly. He became my savior, my protector. We've been in love ever since. My story has a very happy ending. I wouldn't change the past because it led me to your father. I believe he's the man I was supposed to be with. Not once did he view me as a victim or damaged goods. He loved me like I'd never suffered a day in my life."

I took a deep breath, feeling the pain in my chest. I still wanted to cry, still wanted to break down. "You didn't deserve that. No woman does…" Before I could stop them, tears fell from my eyes.

My father watched me, his eyes softening.

Mama reached her hand across the table and placed it on mine. "Please don't cry for me, sweetheart. That time in my life has no hold over me anymore. It has no power whatsoever. I defeated my past, have found love and beauty in this world that can never be taken away."

"I know. But it…it's just wrong."

"And I got my justice," she said. "I killed him myself. I've never felt any remorse for it."

"You shouldn't…" I knew Bones hated us for taking his father away, but he was a bad man who'd deserved to die. He'd deserved something worse than death. "You should have tortured him and made him beg for death.

184

You should have ripped all his organs out until there was nothing left."

Mama squeezed my hand. "He's gone now, so it doesn't matter. But I hope you understand why accepting Griffin has been so difficult for both of us. We haven't said his father's name in almost thirty years… because it was banned from this house. This man wanted to hurt us as well, and only his love for you changed his mind. It's hard for me to look at him and not think of what his father did to me. It's even worse for your father, who also lost his sister. You're asking a lot of us, and I hope our attempt shows how much you mean to us."

"It does…absolutely."

She pulled her hand away. "We wanted you to know, to understand the entire situation."

"I do," I said. "And I know it must be hard for you. It would be hard for me. Sometimes I have nightmares about Knuckles. If I had to interact with that man again, I'd be sick to my stomach. But the issue with Griffin is… he's not his father."

My father wore the same cold look on his face.

My mother sighed quietly. "I know…"

"I'm not being insensitive because I understand just how painful that was for you," I said gently. "I understand why this man isn't your first choice. I understand why you wish I'd fallen for someone else. If I didn't love him as much as I do, I would just throw in the towel and find love elsewhere. But what we have together…it's stronger than love. I'm so sorry that I'm putting you through this. Truly. But I have to fight for him."

My mother gave a slight nod. "I understand."

"And you said Father kept you as a prisoner…what does that mean?" Was that any different from what Bones did to me?

"My relationship with your father is private," she said, doing her best not to sound harsh. "Don't compare our relationship to yours, and don't validate your decisions based on our past. This man has admitted he wanted to hurt us. Your father never had a vendetta against me."

I felt the sternness in her tone, so I didn't press it. "I understand."

My father moved his hand from her back and grabbed her hand on the table. I didn't fail to see the similarities between them and my relationship with Bones. My father was silent and stern just the way Bones was. They looked nothing alike, but their natures were identical. "I think one of the reasons I've fallen for Griffin is because he's very similar to you. Aggressive, protective, domineering…stubborn as hell. You always wanted me to be with a strong man. You've been around him long enough to know he's the strongest man out there."

"But I'm afraid he'll use that strength against you—all of us." My father finally spoke after a long bout of silence. "I'm also looking for a man that's loyal. Loyalty is the most important thing in this world."

"He is loyal," I said quietly. "Extremely. And he's honest. He'll tell you the truth—even if it hurts you to listen to it. He doesn't care for bullshit, and he won't change himself for anyone. That's what I love about him. He's not afraid to be who he is—all the good and the bad. You know exactly what you're getting from him, so if he says he's loyal, then he's loyal."

My father gave a slight nod. "I need more time to decide how I feel about him."

"Me too," Mama whispered.

It'd been almost six weeks since I'd introduced Bones to them for the first time. It seemed like a lifetime. I wanted to let my guard down, to finally be happy knowing I got to keep the man I loved. This torture never seemed to end. "How much more time?"

Instantly, the rage exploded out of my father. "Are you in a hurry?" my father snapped. "You're lucky we're even considering him. Don't push it, Vanessa."

"I wasn't trying to sound pushy. I just want to know if you'll ever come to a decision. Because it seems like you're going to distrust him no matter how much time has passed."

"You're right," Father said. "We probably will never really trust him."

"But we may be able to accept him and give him a chance to earn our trust," Mama said. "We'll take it one day at a time. You don't have to stay here in the process. Griffin has been a tremendous help at the winery, but proving how hard he can work isn't what's important to us. You're what's important to us."

"No, we'll stay a little longer," I said. "He's not

working hard to prove how strong he is. He's trying to prove how much he'll sacrifice for a real chance, for the possibility of sharing a drink with you and having a real conversation. That's what he's trying to prove...that he'll do anything for me."

EIGHT

Bones

I sat in the truck and watched the sun move to the horizon. The heat was a lot more apparent in Tuscany than it was in the northern part of the country. I could feel it in the rays that pierced through the window. With my arm hanging out over the side, I watched the Tuscan fields move gently in the soft breeze.

I knew what they were discussing inside the house. Vanessa already knew about her mother, but the conversation would be painful to endure. At least the secret would be out, and they could move on with their lives—as a family.

An hour went by, and she finally came out and walked to the truck. She got inside and then immediately scooted over until she was right up against me. She rested her head against my shoulder and linked her arm through mine. Without saying a single word, she expressed her sorrow.

I started the engine and drove home. I let her lie on me, use me as a crutch. I let her enjoy her silence without being interrogated. I was just grateful she didn't hate me because of what my father did to her mother.

We reached the house then walked inside. Vanessa obviously didn't seem interested in dinner because she went straight to bed. She pulled on one of my t-shirts then crawled under the sheets.

I undressed and joined her, skipping the shower because I knew she wanted me beside her. I lay next to her, staring at her grief-stricken face as my hand moved to her neck. I watched her with a look full of pity, a heart heavy with sadness. I'd never felt anything close to empathy, but this woman brought out sensitive qualities I didn't think I was capable of feeling. When she was in pain, I was in pain. Just as deeply as we were connected when we made love, I was connected to her sadness when she was unhappy.

I could feel it all the way down to my bones.

She stared at me through her thick eyelashes, her green eyes vibrating with pain. Her breathing was slow and deep, pain in every breath she took. Her hand snaked to mine on her neck, and she held it there, feeling my pulse as I felt hers.

"What can I do?" I would do anything to wipe off that sad look on her face. If there was anything I could possibly do to help, I would. If my father were still alive right now, I would kill him myself if that brought her peace.

Her fingertips grazed against mine as she held my gaze. "Make love to me." That seemed to be the only thing she ever wanted from me. She didn't want sex to get off like a lot of other women did. She wanted a slow and passionate connection, the way we held each other as we moved. She wanted me to blanket her with all of me, to cushion her against the harsh realities of life. She wanted to get lost in me, to shut out the outside world altogether. When it was just the two of us, there was nothing that could hurt us. She wanted me for me, not for the way I could make her feel.

"You always want me to make love to you." She never asked me to clean up the house, make dinner, or help her with anything. The only request she voiced was the sexiest phrase I'd ever heard a woman say. It wasn't even a question because I didn't have a choice in the matter. She knew exactly what she wanted, and she wasn't afraid to ask for it.

Like a real woman.

"Yeah?" she whispered. "You want me to ask someone else?"

The corner of my lip rose in a smile. "You'd be disappointed if you did. A boy will never compete with a man."

"I won't ask a boy."

"They're all boys compared to me." I pushed my boxers down and moved on top of her, settling between her legs. Her thong was pulled to the side so I could fit my fat dick between her legs. She was wet but not drenched like she was in the morning. I sank deep inside her, feeling the soft flesh constrict around me. I stopped when I was buried deep within, and I listened to her breathing increase as she felt me stretch her wide apart.

Her hands moved into my hair, and she locked her ankles together. The light burned in her eyes, her arousal increasing as she felt me stretch her as far as possible. She pulled my forehead to hers and squeezed my waist with her thighs. "If you're the only man on the planet…can I keep you forever?"

I pulled my face back to look at her, my thick cock buried deep inside her. A more beautiful woman had never been under me, had never had me so intimately. This woman had snatched my heart out of my chest and never returned it. "Always." I rubbed my nose against hers, pledging my heart to her for the rest of time. Even if I couldn't keep her, she would always have all of me.

Her eyes softened as she looked at me, her hand sliding to my cheek. "I want you for the rest of my life…"

I turned into her hand and kissed her palm, tasting her and smelling her. I was the luckiest man in the world, to be buried between her legs and listen to her love me so openly. Her love didn't scare me, nor her pledge of forever. Most men ran from commitment, weren't man enough to handle a woman's love. But I could handle hers so easily, could thrive in it. I wasn't the least bit scared. I'd seen the world; I knew what was out there.

Nothing compared to her.

"Baby, promise me something." I started to move

inside her, taking her slowly. "If this works, promise me you'll marry me." I couldn't get down on one knee and ask for her hand at that moment. I didn't have a ring or a proposal planned, but I didn't need any of those things. However, I did need her family's permission.

Her hand slowly trailed down my face, and the softness in her eyes deepened into an emotional look. Her eyes watered, a thin film of moisture over the surface of her gaze. She took a breath, her lips parting as she nearly gasped in surprise. "Yes."

I NEVER TOLD Vanessa about my conversation with her father.

When he basically asked me to leave my job for good.

I would concede if he granted me acceptance into the family. But he didn't do that, refusing to give me an answer.

He asked me to make a sacrifice when I didn't even know if it would count for anything. It would be stupid to walk away from my business and give it up, and then hear her parents tell me I wasn't good enough for their daughter.

It had to be fair.

When we went to the winery the next day, Vanessa was still quiet. All she craved was the peace and easiness her family used to provide. Life used to be simple, and her family was her home base. But now it was the most stressful part of her life. If she wanted it to return to normal, she just had to get rid of me.

But she refused to do that.

She was loyal to me, seeing this all the way through. And I was loyal to her, putting up with every hurdle to stay in the race.

I walked past the main building and followed the cobblestone pathway toward the warehouse where I would slave away for the next eight hours. When I was halfway there, a woman stepped out in high-rise jeans with a white top that tied in the front at her belly. Tall, slender, and with thick brown hair that trailed to her shoulders, she didn't look like she belonged there, especially in her nude pumps.

Her eyes settled on me, and she watched me as she came closer, her green eyes almost identical to Vanessa's. She wore a stern expression, her thoughts not written on her face the way Vanessa's were.

She was a Barsetti. No doubt about it.

She stopped in front of me, one hand on her hip. She sized me up and down, looking at me like I was livestock about to be judged. "Griffin, right?"

"Yes." I stayed five feet away from her and didn't bother extending my hand to shake hers. I hadn't shaken hands with a single Barsetti, not even Vanessa. That was a privilege I hadn't earned yet, and I probably never would.

"Carmen. Nice to meet you."

She seemed to be the only Barsetti who wasn't openly hostile toward me. Her loosely curled hair framed her face, and her slender appearance made her fit to be on the runway. There was something in the Barsetti blood that made their men handsome and their women beautiful. She had a lot of similarities to Vanessa, but her features were also distinctly different. Her mother must be a little more exotic than Pearl. "Yes. Nice to meet you. Are you Cane's daughter?"

"Yes." She tilted her head slightly as she studied me. "My father hates you. Like, really hates you."

I hoped she didn't expect that to hurt my feelings. "I picked up on that."

"He's a bit of a psychopath when it comes to the family. Don't take it too personally."

"No, it is personal." Extremely personal.

"Vanessa told me she's hung up on you. I grew up with her, so I've known about every guy she's liked and every crush she's ever had. When I hear her talk about you, I know it's different. I know it's real. So…I'm rooting for you."

Wow, that was a nice change. "Thanks."

She stepped closer to me, moving her hands into her back pockets. "My father is impossible to win over. So don't spend your time getting him to like you. Plus, he hates a kiss-ass. There are some people who will love you no matter what you do, and there are other people who will never love you no matter what you do…and he's the latter. Focus on Crow. My uncle is a lot more practical."

I liked her bluntness. "Thanks for the heads-up."

"I think it's sweet you're trying so hard to win them

over for Vanessa. I know my family is terrifying, so it's a big statement on your part."

Now, I really liked her.

"Just the fact that you care enough tells me you're worth our time." She extended her hand to shake mine. "If you ever need any advice, let me know."

The corner of my mouth rose in a smile before I reached for her hand. "Thanks."

"Carmen." Cane's stern voice shattered the pleasant conversation we were having. He emerged out of the second warehouse, wearing a gray V-neck and black jeans. It wasn't clear who he was angrier at, me or Carmen. He flashed her a hostile look before he placed his body in between us.

I rolled my eyes because I couldn't stop myself. He actually thought I was going to strangle his daughter on the cobblestone walkway?

Cane caught the look. "You wanna die, asshole?" He shoved me hard in the chest.

I stepped back, not because of his push, but because getting away from him was the best way to defuse his anger. "Just saying hello."

He shoved me again.

I clenched my jaw and forced myself back, doing my best not to rise to his anger. I wanted to break his fist with my chest. If he hit me again, I wanted to slam his body down onto the stone sidewalk and crack his skull open.

Vanessa. I had to focus on the reward. If I retaliated, it would make it that much harder to win over her family.

I could take a beating if I got to spend my life with the one woman I loved. It wasn't much to sacrifice.

"Father." Carmen grabbed him by the arm and pulled him back. "Knock it off. I started talking to him." Even in her five-inch heels, she was a foot shorter than him. The Barsetti men were tall, reaching my height.

"I don't give a shit." He pushed her off and came at me again.

This time, I stepped out of the way and held my hands up. "Get your shit together, man. Just saying hi."

"What the fuck did you say to me?" He puffed up his chest and came after me again.

I kept my hands up, ready to stop his fist when he threw a punch.

"Father!" Carmen slammed her heel down. "Knock it off now, or I'll tell Mama and she'll be down here in two seconds to shove her foot up your ass."

Cane stilled at the threat, the anger disappearing from his eyes for a brief second.

I tried not to smile at Carmen's insult, loving the way she had a mouth on her like Vanessa.

Cane was the kind of man who wasn't afraid of anything, but the mention of his petite wife made him hit the brakes. He kept his gaze on me, but his hands lowered to his sides. "Stay away from my daughter, alright? You wanna talk? Talk to me or Crow. Stay the fuck away from my daughter. Don't even fucking look at her. I'll shoot you between the eyes if you come within twenty feet of her."

Carmen rolled her eyes. "Oh my god, Father. Chill

out. I was the one who talked to him. He didn't even look twice at me."

Cane didn't care about any of that. "Go." He barked like a dog and pointed to the warehouse. "Get to work, you piece of shit."

I lowered my hands and walked around him, heading to the warehouse.

Carmen spoke once my back was turned. "You need to calm the hell down. He was nothing but nice to me."

"Not now, Carmen," Cane barked. "I don't want you anywhere near him. He's a piece of shit, and I don't like him."

"Well, I don't like you." Carmen's heels clapped against the cobblestone as she walked off.

I smiled before I stepped inside the warehouse, appreciating my new ally. It was novel to be treated as a human being for once, to be seen as a person rather than a murderer and a criminal. Carmen was the first one to give me a fresh start, to accept me because Vanessa loved me.

It was a nice change.

IT WAS late afternoon when Crow stepped inside the warehouse. He moved to the desk in the corner, flipped through the paperwork, and then made a phone call. Speaking in Italian, he spoke with one of his clients about the distribution of the wine to the right location.

I could speak Italian, so I understood every word. But I kept working, putting the crates on the dolly and transferring the cargo to the appropriate sections. The place had a central cooling system to keep the wine at the perfect temperature, but I always ran hot, so I was constantly sweating in my t-shirts and jeans.

Crow hung up then walked toward me. "One of the trucks is coming early tomorrow. All the crates need to be finished before you leave today."

I'd been working my ass off for weeks, and not once did I get any respect for it. They treated me like a dog, expecting me to do the grunt work with a smile on my face. Now he'd asked me to work later even though I was the most efficient worker they had. "That didn't sound like a question." I knew I shouldn't be a smartass, but my temper was rising. I'd been making every sacrifice to be given a real chance, but nothing was ever good enough for them. We'd been here for weeks, but they should have made their decision within a few days.

Crow turned to me, his dark eyes cold. "Because it wasn't." With straight shoulders and perfect posture, he challenged me.

"I did my time today. If you want me to stay longer, you need to ask."

He cocked an eyebrow, baffled by my attitude. "Your stupidity continues to surprise me."

"It's not stupidity, it's respect. I'm willing to work hard for what I want, but I'm not a goddamn doormat. Treat me like a human being. I've earned that much over the last six weeks. Would you want your daughter to be with a man who acts like a slave? That's not me, and you should be grateful that it's not." I wiped my palms together, soothing my blisters underneath the dirt.

Crow didn't blink as he examined me. As if his features were carved out of ice, he was impossible to decipher. If he didn't want you to know what he was thinking, he'd make sure you couldn't figure it out.

"I'll do anything for your daughter—except act like your bitch." I'd already proven myself to this family. Now it was up to them to see my worth. I had to stand up for myself, because if I didn't, why should they believe I'd stand up for their daughter?

Crow came closer to me, his muscular arms resting by his sides. "I'm sorry about my brother. His temper is worse than mine."

That was better. "Apology accepted."

"But you should stay away from Carmen," he said. "Going anywhere near his daughter is not the best way to get on his good side."

"She talked to me."

"Doesn't matter." His black shirt was tight around his muscular physique, stretching over his biceps. His hair was dark like his clothes, and his green eyes looked like broken shards of green glass. "Take my advice or don't. I don't give a shit." He closed the gap between us until we were close together.

"Vanessa was upset for the rest of the night…after your family conversation."

He crossed his arms over his chest. "My wife was too."

"But she still doesn't look at me the way you do," I said. "She doesn't look at me like I'm my father. I hope someday you can too…because I'm sincerely sorry for what my father did to your family." It didn't matter whether he believed me or not. My sincerity was real. "It hurts me to see Vanessa in pain. I feel what she feels, and knowing she's hurt over what happened to your wife and aunt…kills me inside. I'm immune to pain and emotion, but Vanessa is an exception to that. That's how I knew I loved her…because I could feel everything she felt."

Crow stared at me with his stoic expression again, refusing to give me any insight into his thoughts. He shifted his weight to one leg, and his black wedding ring matched his dark clothes. The scruff was coming in along his face, like he hadn't shaved in a while. He suddenly stepped back, his arms still across his chest. "Would you mind staying later and helping me with these crates?"

It was the sun piercing a cloudy sky, a sign of hope in a storm. It was one of the rare times when Crow was civil to me, treating me like a man instead of an enemy. The more I stood my ground, the more he respected me. "Not in the least."

"I LIKE YOUR COUSIN."

Vanessa sat across from me at the dining table and ate the dinner I'd prepared. "Carmen? You saw her today?"

"We crossed paths."

"Yeah, she's great." She grabbed her wineglass by the stem and took a drink. "She's a little older than me and much sassier…if you can believe it."

No, I couldn't. Vanessa was the biggest spitfire I'd ever met.

"She said she was rooting for me…nice change."

"I told her how I felt about you. She knows I've never really felt anything for any of the men in my life. They were just…ways to pass the time. So when I told her I wanted to spend my life with you, she was immediately on my side. She seems to trust my instincts more than everyone else in the family."

"It's not a matter of trusting your instincts." Her family's distrust annoyed me, but they were right to be cautious around me. I would judge them if they dropped their guard any sooner. "It's a matter of overcoming their hatred. And trust me, that's not easy to do…" I only spared her family because my love for her blacked out everything else.

"But still…it's been six weeks. They need to get over it."

That was something I could agree on. "True." I didn't have wine with dinner because I preferred stronger booze. I'd have wine if we went to a fancy restaurant or we were dining with her family, but when it was just the two of us, I continued my habits because she accepted me completely. "Your uncle caught me talking to Carmen and flipped out."

She dropped her fork. "Please tell me he didn't hit you again."

Did pushing me count? "No."

She sighed in relief. "Good…I'd kick his ass if he did."

"Just told me to stay away from her."

She rolled her eyes. "My uncle is very sweet and affectionate. I think he's more emotional than my father, but he doesn't understand how to control it or express it. He just wants to keep Carmen safe, but then he flips out and makes a situation out of nothing…"

"Yes, he's a bit dramatic."

"Thanks for being understanding. And not just with him…but with everything." She looked down at her food, like she was embarrassed that I had to put up with so much bullshit with her family.

My hand moved to hers on the table. "You're worth it, baby."

She lifted her gaze and gave me the kind of look I lived for, like I was her hero. I was the one thing she was living for, the man who earned her complete devotion and affection. Her small fingers wrapped around mine, and she squeezed my hand in response, like words weren't enough to express what she was feeling.

I held her hand on the table, feeling the never-ending connection between us. White-hot and smoldering, our love burned without gasoline to feed off of. The fire continued to roar, unable to be doused with water or anything else. I knew what we had was special because I could always feel it, no matter how good or bad our situation was. It was a love built over time, a love that defied the impossible. She should hate me, but she didn't. And I should have killed her but never could. I didn't believe in fate or soul mates. I didn't even believe in love. But Vanessa made me reconsider everything.

My phone started to vibrate in my pocket, but I ignored it because nothing seemed more important than her, than this.

She pulled her hand away. "It's okay. Answer it." She grabbed her fork again and tilted her head toward her food. She didn't seem angry at the disturbance, knowing I rarely got phone calls. And when I did, they were usually important.

I took the call when I saw Max's name on the screen. "What?" I excused myself from the table and headed to our bedroom down the hall.

Max didn't seem surprised by my greeting. "Shane had a mission in India, and it went well. So he's back to active duty."

"That's great. Good for him."

"I encouraged him to stay home longer, but he said he was going crazy with Cynthia waiting on him all the time."

I grinned. "Sounds about right." I sat in the armchair next to the bed, my long legs stretched out before me. I eyed the bed, thinking about the way I took

Vanessa that morning. With her flat on her belly, I held myself on top of her and fucked her into the mattress, getting deep inside her. "Did you call me just to say that?"

"Right to the point, huh?"

"I'm having dinner with my woman."

"Then why did you answer the phone?" he countered.

My eyes narrowed even though I wasn't looking at him. "She told me to."

"When did you start listening to other people?"

If he were in the room, I'd smack him upside the head. "I'm hanging up now."

He laughed, knowing he'd pushed my buttons. "I have a job for you. Australia. You need to leave tomorrow."

I couldn't do that right now. "I'm in the middle of something, Max. Send one of the other guys."

"We've already rotated twice," he said. "I know you're off in Tuscany trying to kiss Barsetti ass, but we've got a business to run. If you won't jump on this, I'll have to go. And I just got back from Russia yesterday."

Since they'd already rotated twice to give me the time off, I couldn't ask them to give me any more time. It would be unfair, and I would be taking advantage of our friendship instead of being professional. "I'll do it, then."

"Good. I'll send you all the documents. It's a low-key hit. Shouldn't be any complications."

"Good. Vanessa's father will be pissed if I come back with another gunshot wound."

"Didn't realize he gave a damn."

"He doesn't. He just doesn't like how my job involves Vanessa."

"I don't think he needs to worry about that," he said. "Our security is pretty tight."

"He doesn't agree."

"I hate to be the bearer of bad news, but I don't think this is going to end well…"

There were good days and bad days. Today, Crow wasn't nearly as hostile as he usually was. But tomorrow, he could flip on me again. "That makes two of us."

I KNEW Vanessa was going to be angry about my leaving, so I purposely kept it from her until after the evening sex was over. On her hands and knees on the bed, she had her ass in my face as I stood at the foot of the bed.

I gripped her hips and thrust into her hard, pounding into that wet slit and driving myself deep inside her. I was welcomed by her tightness and warmth, the soft flesh of her perfect pussy.

These were my favorite moments, when it was quiet in the bedroom with the exception of our deep breathing, our pants, and her sexy moans. She said my name from time to time, right before she hit her climax. It was animalistic, carnal, and lustful.

Exactly how it should be.

I fucked a woman I also loved, and that made the sex even better.

I sucked my thumb before I pushed it into her asshole, getting inside that tight little hole that was staring back at me. I loved to watch it while I fucked her from behind, to see her muscles shift underneath her olive skin. Her dark hair was beautiful, and her perky ass was a gorgeous sight.

She tensed when she felt my finger, having never felt it before. "What are you doing?"

My fingers gripped her cheek while my thumb moved in and out. I felt her hole tighten around me, grip my thumb. "Trust me."

"Griffin…"

"I said, trust me." I kept fucking her while I fingered her, feeling my cock slide in and out against my thumb. She slowly loosened around me, and I could hear her breathing change as she got used to the intrusion in her rear. She was tight, even just around my thumb. I wondered if she could handle my fat dick.

She gripped the sheets, and her moans became deeper and louder. Her back arched, and her cunt tightened around my dick. Her asshole clenched around my thumb. Before her screams emerged, I knew she was coming. "Griffin…" She thrust back into me, sheathing my dick over and over as the cream built up along the base. "God…"

My chest began to ache from the deep breaths I started to take. The image in front of me was so erotic, so sexy, that my dick started to throb inside her. I wanted to last longer and make her come again, but my dick had other plans. I pushed my thumb farther inside her as my dick started to pulse. I dumped all my come inside her, filling her channel with my white seed. I moaned under my breath as I enjoyed every single second of the high, every single moment of the intense pleasure.

When I finished, I pulled my dick out to watch my come seep out of her entrance. Bright against her dark skin, my seed dripped down her wet pussy. Watching my explosion drip from her opening made me feel like a man, like I'd truly accomplished something.

I washed up before I came back to bed. She didn't clean herself up because she knew I didn't want her to. Even if my come got all over the sheets, I liked having my essence sit inside her all night long.

I got into bed beside her, seeing the heaviness in her eyes. After sex, she usually went to sleep right away. She slid against my side and cuddled beside me, her arm draped over my waist. She smelled like her perfume, sex, and me.

The perfect scent.

"I love you," she said with a sigh, her eyes closing. She usually said it right before she went to sleep.

"I love you too." My fingers slid through her hair, feeling the soft strands that tickled my chest in the middle of the night.

She tucked her leg in between mine, wrapping around me like a snake.

"Baby?"

"Hmm?"

"I'm leaving in the morning."

She immediately stilled at my words, and when she didn't ask where I was going, I knew she'd figured out exactly why I had to leave. She slowly sat up so she could look down at me. "You can't leave right now, Griffin. It's the worst time."

"I know, but I don't have a choice."

"You always have a choice. You never do anything you don't want to do."

"This is different. I'm sorry, baby."

The disappointment in her eyes made me feel like shit. "Have one of the other guys go."

"They've already rotated twice. I tried to get out of it, baby. But I can't abandon my obligations for you."

She sighed as she dragged her hand down my chest. "The timing couldn't be worse."

"I know…"

"I don't want to tell my parents you had to leave. We can't give them any excuse to dislike you."

"I know that too. But this is how it has to be. I'll come back as soon as I can, and maybe they'll see how simple the process really is."

She stared at my chest, unable to fight her disappointment. "My parents hate what you do."

"Yeah, I know." Her father made it clear how much he despised it.

She lowered herself back to my chest and returned her arm around my torso. She went quiet, knowing saying anything more wouldn't change the outcome. I'd made my decision, and I had to leave even if I didn't want to. "How long will you be gone?"

"A few days. I'm going to Australia."

She stayed quiet, her hair stretching across my body. "I understand your work is important to you, but when we have our own family, you won't be able to do it anymore. It would be hard enough for me to lose you if you never came back…but it would be so much worse on our children. You know what it's like to grow up without parents. Don't do that to your own family." She squeezed me tighter, like I might slip away any moment.

Vanessa knew I wanted to marry her. But we never talked about having a family. I'd never considered having children. It didn't seem possible, so I never entertained the idea. Being a father seemed strange to me. I wouldn't even know where to start. I lived a life of solitude, and I could hardly communicate with people. Vanessa and the boys seemed to be the only people who understood me. "We'll cross that bridge when we come to it."

Vanessa lifted her head again to look at me, the disappointment gone. Now she looked stern and serious, like I'd said something that pissed her off. "Griffin, I need to have children. That's nonnegotiable."

I could picture her as a mother, giving them activities and teaching them how to paint. I could also see her being the disciplinarian, making them into strong and independent adults. I could see her loving them the way my mother loved me, wearing her heart on her sleeve with a smile on her lips.

"So don't ask me to marry you unless that's something you want…"

She was willing to do anything to make this relationship work, to spend six weeks trying to get her family to like me even though our mutual hatred ran so deep. But that wasn't our breaking point. This was. "Okay."

"Okay what?" she whispered, hesitation in her eyes.

"I won't ask you if I don't want a family."

Fear moved into her gaze, like she was afraid to ask the question before it came out of her mouth. "Is that something you want…?"

I didn't want to answer with the truth because it was so harsh. I couldn't picture someone like me being a father. But then again, I couldn't picture myself loving someone the way I loved Vanessa. I couldn't picture myself forcing my enemies to like me just so I could keep her. With Vanessa, anything was possible. "All I know is I want you…and I'm willing to do anything to keep you."

"You've never wanted to have your own family?"

I shook my head slightly. "It's never crossed my mind. I didn't think that was an option for me."

"It's always an option."

"We both know I'm not father material."

"You weren't boyfriend material, but look at you now."

"I'm not your boyfriend." I didn't like that label one bit. I was committed to her, and she was committed to me. I loved her with all my heart. A label like that didn't seem to fit us.

"Then what are you?"

"I don't know. But I'm definitely not your boyfriend. I'm more than that. I'm your man. You're my woman."

"Now you're talking like a caveman."

"It gets my point across, at least."

Her lips softened into a smile. "You're very simple."

"I like simple."

She leaned down and pressed a kiss to my chest. "I like it too. But I think you can be anything you want to be. You have the heart to be a great father. I know you do. My father said he wasn't ready to be a parent when my mom was pregnant with Conway, but once Conway arrived, his life changed for the better. Look at the way he is with me…he loves me more than anything. You could be the exact same way."

"I guess."

She lifted her head to look at me again. "I don't want to lose you, Griffin. But I'll walk away if I have to…"

If I managed to work this out with her parents, it would be a waste to ever let her go. "Let's get through this first and revisit that conversation later."

"Alright…" She settled into my chest again and became silent.

I was tired from working in the warehouse all day, but now I couldn't sleep. I stared at the ceiling for the next few hours, thinking about how much my life had changed —and how much more was about to change.

NINE

Vanessa

Bones packed his bag and placed it by the front door. He was taking a taxi to Florence so I could have the truck while he was gone. He didn't say much as he got ready that morning. We did our normal routine, making love as soon as the alarm went off before he showered and got dressed.

Now I stood by the front door, dreading the moment I had to say goodbye to him. I loved spending this time with him in Tuscany with my family. It was a dream come true, something I didn't even know I wanted until I had it. I hadn't missed Milan once.

He carried a pistol in his hand then placed it in my palm. "It's loaded. More rounds in the nightstand."

I gripped the handle and pointed it at the ground.

"But I'm sure you won't need it." He stared down at me, bending his neck because I was so much shorter than him.

I didn't want to sleep in this house alone, not without him there. I felt so exposed, so alone. "I think I'm going to stay with my parents."

Bones didn't take the gun away from me. "You should keep it anyway. Put it in your nightstand."

"Alright." I set the gun on the entryway table then crossed my arms over my chest.

"This area is perfectly safe, baby. You don't need to stay with your parents."

"I want to. I know it's stupid, but I can't sleep without you here. I used to do it all the time when I was single. I was never scared of anything. Even after Knuckles, I was fine. But when you came into my life, everything changed. I hate it when you're gone…" I didn't want to whine or complain about his job, but I couldn't lie about the way his absence made me feel. My life was turned upside down when he was gone.

His fingers moved under my chin, and he lifted my gaze to meet his. "I hate it when I'm gone too. I worry about you as much as you worry about me."

"I doubt that…" He was the one directly putting himself at risk. He was sent off to kill someone, and I was always afraid someone would kill him instead. If Max ever called me and told me Bones would never return, I wouldn't know how to go on. "I told my father you would stop doing this if I asked you to…" Bones had never said those words to me, had always told me how much his work meant to him. It was his life, and he didn't just do it for the money. He needed it for his anger, needed it to give him purpose.

He stared at me, his callused fingers rough against my smooth skin. His blue eyes showed his undying affection for me, but there was also a hint of a resistance. His wide shoulders were twice my length, and his arms were thick enough to be tree trunks. His size always made me feel smaller, even smaller than I really was.

"Was I right…?"

His fingers slid down my neck until his hand gripped my waist. He moved into me, his chin moving on top of my head. He pulled me close to him, holding me in the doorway. His fingers gripped the back of my t-shirt, keeping me in place like I might float away. "Yes." He pressed a kiss to the top of my head. "But please don't ask me. Don't ask me to give up my livelihood, my purpose. I would never ask you to stop painting."

"Painting isn't dangerous."

"Doesn't matter." He pulled away so he could look at me again.

"If my parents accept us and we move forward…it's inevitable. I can't handle you doing this forever. I can't suffer every single moment you're gone. Don't turn me into Cynthia. Don't come back to me in worse condition than when you left."

When he sighed, it sounded more like a growl. "I've done nothing but make sacrifices for this relationship."

"I know you have… I know."

"You're asking me to give up everything…all that I am."

"And embrace everything else. You aren't giving up anything, Griffin. You're growing into a new man. That's all."

"Sounds like the same thing to me."

"It's not." My arms rested on his. "I'm not asking you to make the sacrifice now, but if you're my husband, you'll have to do it. I can't live like that. Don't make me live like that…please." I rested my forehead against his chest and closed my eyes. "I love you so much…"

He cupped the back of my head and rested his lips against my forehead. "I know you do, baby."

I squeezed him with my arms, wanting to hold on to him as long as I could. Once he was gone, I wouldn't speak to him for almost a week. Every day would feel like an eternity until he was back in my arms. "Please call me when you're on your way back."

"I'll try. But if I don't, that doesn't mean anything is wrong." He pulled away and grabbed his bag from the floor. "I'll always come back to you, baby. I'll always do everything I can to make it back to where I belong."

I wasn't going to cry because it was pathetic. I'd never been the kind of woman to cry, to let tears streak down my face. I preferred to keep my feelings bottled up inside and forget they existed. I preferred to respond to my pain with smartass comments and sassiness. But with Bones, I couldn't do that. He stripped away my exterior until the wall surrounding my heart was long gone. Now all that was left was me…just me.

The tears started, and I couldn't stop them.

He stared at me, his eyes hurt and his jaw clenched in pain. "Baby…"

I wiped my tears away with my fingertips and sniffed. "I'm sorry."

"Don't be sorry. Just don't cry." He cupped my cheeks and kissed my tears away, absorbing them with his lips. "I'll be back. I promise."

"You can't make a promise like that."

"Yes, I can. Because nothing will ever stop me from coming back to you."

WHEN I GOT to the winery, I had my bags of clothes in the truck along with the pistol Bones gave to me. I intended to drive to my parents' place once the workday was over and ask if I could crash there for a few days. That house made me feel safe because my father made sure nothing ever happened to us, and it also chased away the loneliness from my man's absence.

I headed into the main building and walked to my father's office. He was usually there as soon as the sun rose, wanting to get his job done so he could run along the fields and then hit his private gym.

I knocked on the door before I stepped inside. "Can I come in?"

"Why do you always ask me that?" my father asked as he made notes with his pen. "When have you ever asked that and I said no?"

Not once. "Never."

"Exactly." He kept writing. "What do you need, *tesoro*?" He finished his note then set down his pen. He leaned back in the leather armchair and looked up at me, his gaze hard like he anticipated I had something important to say about Bones. But then his gaze softened, and the concern started to come into his expression. "*Tesoro*, what is it? Everything alright?" He shifted from being a man to being a father instantly.

"Yeah, I'm fine." I cleared my throat. "Would it be okay if I stayed with you and Mama for a few days?"

My father's eyes shifted back and forth slightly as he looked at me. His wide shoulders seemed to slacken, and the pain on his face mirrored the sadness in my heart. When I saw him interact with others, he didn't show the slightest hint of empathy or compassion, but with me, when I was in pain, he was devastated. "Our home is always your home, *tesoro*. But what happened with Griffin?"

"He had to leave for a job…he'll be back in a few days." I thought I did a better job of hiding my sadness, but my father could see right through my stoic expression. I'd cried before Bones left, so my eyes were probably still red and puffy.

The sadness disappeared from his gaze, replaced by annoyance and disappointment. "I see…"

"I just don't like being alone when he's not there."

My father rested his fingertips against his lips, looking at me without really seeing me. He seemed to be thinking something else. "I'm trying to like this man, but when you tell me this, it's hard not to hate him. It's hard not to hate him when he hurts my daughter."

"He's not hurting me. He's just…"

"Leaving you and risking his life," he countered. "And making you worry until you're sick to your stomach. He's leaving you alone and defenseless. A man never does that to his woman. It makes me respect him less."

"Did you respect him in the first place?"

He rubbed his fingers over his chin. "A little."

"Well, he said he would stop if I asked him to…but he doesn't want me to ask."

My father dropped his hands into his lap. "So, you're never going to?"

"No. I told him this has to stop if he wants to marry me, especially when we start a family."

My father cocked his head slightly, his eyes narrowing. "You talk about that sort of thing?"

I nodded. "Of course."

"And you really think he'll stop?"

"He would never lie to me. And he's already sacrificed so much for me…I don't think there's anything he wouldn't do."

My father stared at me, his moss-green eyes deep and indecipherable. If we were having a conversation about something else, he would have been a lot more open and vulnerable. But since Bones was involved, he closed up like a clam.

"Father?"

He released a quiet sigh, as if he anticipated the next thing I was going to say. "Yes?"

I looked him straight in the eye, holding my ground in his office. I couldn't take this indecision anymore, couldn't handle the painful anticipation of his decision. "I need this man in my life as much as I need you. I need you to accept him. I need him…in ways I can't explain. So I'm not waiting for your answer anymore. He's my life. He's my present, my future…he'll be my husband and the father of my kids. That's the end of my story."

He stared at me, his body so still it was like he wasn't breathing. Time seemed to slow down as I waited for a response, waited for him to yell at me or accept what I said. The sun was bright outside his window, but the mood in his office was dark and cold. His jaw was clenched, and his eyes were hollow. It didn't seem like he would say anything at all because the silence spanned several minutes.

Just when I turned to walk out, he spoke.

"Okay."

I turned back to my father, shocked by the single word he'd just uttered. I had to stare at him to make sure I'd really heard it, that it wasn't a dream I fabricated myself. "Really…?"

He nodded. "Really."

CARMEN SAT across from me at the restaurant, her high cheekbones amplified by the blush that outlined her feminine facial features. Tall and thin, she had luscious brown hair like her mother's. She had Barsetti olive skin and startling green eyes. She was model material, but she never seemed interested in the runway despite her connections. "This might piss you off a little bit, but I have to say it. Your man is h-o-t. Yes, I had to spell out each letter to get my point across." She had an iced tea in front of her along with a slice of bread she hadn't touched.

I wasn't mad at all. Carmen was my friend and my cousin. She would never stab me in the back or try to cross the line. "I know he is. He's a very gorgeous man."

"Where the hell did you find him? I never meet guys like that. Was he at the military tank store?"

I chuckled. "He found me. And I've never met a man like him before either. Makes every other guy look like a boy in comparison…" And not just because he told me that. He proved it, time and time again.

"I've met a lot of boys too," she said with a sigh. "They don't know what they want…how to handle a woman…how to please a woman." She rolled her eyes. "Most of them are all talk, and when it gets down to the action, they don't know what the hell they're doing."

"Haven't had much luck in the dating world, then?"

"Did my bitterness not give you a clue?" she asked

sarcastically. "I haven't come close to finding the right guy. And even if I did, I'm not sure any of them would be brave enough to face my father. My father is like a wild animal that can't be tamed by anyone but my mother. Impulsive, angry, and ridiculous, he can't stay calm for anything. If I even mentioned a guy, he wanted to interrogate him and his entire family. I know your father is protective of you…but my father is at a whole new level."

"Yeah…I've noticed."

"Nothing would make my father happier than committing me to a nunnery," she said with a chuckle.

"I doubt that. He wants grandkids."

"I think he would prefer it if I were alone rather than for me to have children." She stirred her drink with her straw before she took a sip. "Griffin handled my father pretty well. My father was a dick to him, but he never retaliated."

"He can control his temper…sometimes."

"I think if he's willing to go through all of this for you, then he must really love you. And if he really loves you, I don't think the past matters. I hope our family sees it that way after a while."

Carmen was the only Barsetti who didn't hate Bones. Sapphire didn't hate him either, but since her fiancé did, she couldn't be openly supportive. My cousin was all I had. "I talked to my father this morning…and he said he accepted him."

"Really?" she asked in surprise. "What changed his mind?"

"I don't know. I pretty much demanded for him to accept Griffin, so maybe that was it."

"It's been six weeks," she said. "They should have made up their mind a long time ago. Griffin must be relieved."

I had no way to contact him, so he didn't have a clue. "He doesn't know."

"Why haven't you told him?"

"He's in the field right now. He's unreachable." I was happy my father finally said yes, but my happiness was masked by my fear. If Griffin didn't come home, I wouldn't know what to do with myself. He was my whole life. Every moment that he wasn't beside me was torture. If anyone ever hurt him, I'd grab every gun I could find and hunt down his killers.

"For how long?"

I shrugged. "Until he decides to call."

Carmen gave me a sad look. "That's pretty scary."

"I hate it. I hate it so much. He told me he would stop if I asked…but he asked me not to ask. But I don't think I can do this again. When he gets back, I'm going to tell him I can't handle it anymore. It's too painful."

"I think that's reasonable. My mom would never allow my father to do that."

"My mom wouldn't either. It's a sacrifice he has to make…and I know he'll make it."

"When do you think he'll be back?"

"A few days," I whispered. "I hope it's less. I'm staying with my parents in the meantime."

"Well, he'll be thrilled when he gets back. Finally having your parents' permission will be a relief to him."

Yes, it would be. He battled his frustrations and took my father's insults in stride, even though he would have killed anyone else who disrespected him like that. Bones was a hard man, and violence was the only solution he could conceive of. But he put aside his rage and focused on winning me—even though he had to swallow so much bullshit in the process. "Yeah, it will. He'll finally realize it was all worth it."

"Babe." She placed her hand on mine. "Even if your parents said no, he would still think it was worth it."

I smiled at her, knowing she was right.

"I hope one day I find a man who will battle hell for me, the way he does for you."

"You will, Carmen. And you'll meet him when you least expect it."

IT WAS nice to be home again, in the place that harbored so many wonderful childhood memories. The three-story mansion was too big for the four of us, but it somehow felt like the perfect size when we all lived there.

I was back in my old room, my clothes and necessities with me. My queen-size bed seemed too big for me alone. Without Bones beside me, that bed would never be comfortable. I slept in it for so many years, but now it didn't feel the way it used to.

Now my bed was Bones. His chest, his stomach, his entire physique was my mattress.

I kept looking at my phone, hoping to see a call or text message. It was stupid to expect anything, especially since Bones never contacted me when he was on his missions. This time wouldn't be any different. I would just have to wait it out.

My phone started to ring, but it was a number I didn't recognize. I answered it, just in case it was him. "Hello?"

"Hey, Vanessa. How are you?"

The masculine voice sounded familiar, but I couldn't figure out how I recognized it. "Fine…who is this?"

"You're kidding me, right?" he asked, slightly angry. "I've called you before. You didn't think I was important enough to be added to your contacts?"

After listening to a few more words, I figured it out. "Max?"

"Yes. Took you long enough."

"Sorry. I'll add it this time. Did you need something?"

"No. I'm calling to see if *you* need anything. It's my job, remember? I know you're staying with your parents, but I wanted to check in anyway."

"How did you know that?"

"Bones told me before he left. And I've got your tracker location…"

I didn't mind that Bones had that information, but it felt weird when someone else had it. "Good to know."

"So, let me know if you need anything. I can get to you in two hours if you ever need it."

"I'm not going to need anything, Max. But thanks for offering. By chance…have you talked to him?" He'd only been gone a day, but it felt like a lifetime.

"I just got off the phone with him. He landed in Sydney."

"Oh…how long do you think it'll be before he comes home?"

"Anxious, huh?" he asked with a chuckle. "You remind me of Cynthia."

"I take that as a compliment." I would worry about Bones until he returned, until I could see him in one piece.

"The job is pretty simple. He could be on the flight back in two days. The man needs to sleep."

"Will you check in with him again?"

"I will pretty often, actually. Why?"

"Could you tell him I love him?" He already knew how I felt. I said it when he left, tears streaming down my face. I didn't need to say it now, but I wanted Bones to understand I was thinking about him every moment until he returned.

Max didn't tease me for it. "Yeah, sure."

"Also, tell him he better get back to me in one piece… otherwise, I'll shoot him again."

Max chuckled. "There's the woman he fell so hard for. I'll be sure to tell him." He hung up.

I went downstairs and joined my family for dinner. Lars made chicken piccata, salad, and fresh bread. I sat on one side of the dining table while they sat on the other. My father was dressed down in a gray t-shirt and black sweatpants that hung low on his hips. In some places, his skin hinted at his age, but his youthful physique made him seem fifteen years younger. Mom was dressed in jeans and a t-shirt, what she usually wore around the house.

My father and I hadn't talked since our conversation that morning in his office. It was quiet when I sat down, and we started eating without saying a word to each other. My mom didn't even say anything, and she was the one always trying to make small talk.

"Thanks for letting me stay here." I had to say something to break the silence, to interrupt the awkwardness that settled between us. While this place felt like home, I knew this was their domain now. I'd moved out of the house years ago and started my own life, so my childhood bedroom wasn't mine anymore.

"You don't need to thank us, sweetheart," Mom said. "This will always be your home. Stay as long as you want."

"Stay forever," my father said. "We wouldn't care in the least."

"Be careful what you say," I teased. "This place is pretty big. I could raise a whole family on the second floor, and you wouldn't even know they were there."

"You know how much I want grandkids, so that's fine with me," Mom said. "I would never say this to Conway, but I wish they'd decided to move closer so I could see my grandbaby more often. Milan is just so far away. If we didn't have our winery, we would have left a long time ago to be closer to you two."

"Well, Griffin and I will be here. I don't know about kids right now…but eventually."

My father kept eating despite what I said, but my mother stilled at my words. "You guys intend to move here permanently?"

"He knows that's what I want."

"And did he agree to give it to you?" Mom asked.

I nodded. "He knows how important you are to me. I loved living in Milan, but ever since I've been here, I haven't missed it. Florence is close by, so I could open my gallery there. In the wintertime, we'll probably go to Lake Garda because that's where Griffin likes to spend his winters. But the rest of the time, we can be here."

Whether my mom liked Griffin or not, having me close by would make her dreams come true. She wanted both Conway and me to be right down the road, but just having one of us would be enough. "Your father told me about your conversation this morning…"

"I assumed so. Does that mean you're on board too?"

My father drank his wine and watched the two of us, being an observer of the conversation rather than a participant. He'd already said everything he needed to say, and now my mom was the last one to accept the circumstances.

"I trust your father's instincts," she said. "If he accepts him, then I can accept him too."

The moment was so bittersweet I wasn't sure if I

could handle it. It took so much work to get to this moment, and it finally happened. I only wish Bones were there to see it. "Thank you…it means a lot to me."

"But it'll take a long time for us to trust him," Mom said. "He's welcome in our home and at the winery, and we'll do our best to be kind and respectful. But prejudices like ours don't just disappear. It takes a very long time for serious change to happen."

"That's fine," I said quickly. "That's more than enough. Take your time. Get to know him. Take five years if you need it. I know it'll happen eventually, that you'll love him like a son someday. You'll love him the way you love Sapphire."

"We spoke to your uncle about it," my father said. "He'll behave himself…as best he can."

"Thanks," I whispered. "I know that must have been hard for him."

"The Barsettis are very stubborn and unforgiving," my father said. "But we also love fiercely. We love you more than words can say…and we're willing to do anything to make you happy." He grabbed his wine again and took another drink, his eyes on me. "I just hope you understand the gravity of the situation, the enormous sacrifice we've made for you."

"I do…" Tears almost built up in my eyes, but I made sure they stayed back. "What made you change your mind?" I thought my father would be even more stubborn once Bones was on his mission. I assumed it would make him angry, and he would only hate Bones even more.

My father stared at me for a long time, his gaze more intense than any words he could say. "Seeing how heartbroken you are when he's gone. If he didn't come back, I know how devastated you would be. If you love this man that much, I'm not going to keep him from you. Your mother doesn't want to either."

The air filled my lungs, full of relief and gratitude. My parents may not like the man I chose, but they respected the love I had for him. They loved me enough that they wanted me to be happy, even if my partner was their last choice. "Thank you…for being so understanding. I know this has been hard for you, for all of us. But I promise you that you won't regret it."

"I hope not, sweetheart," Mom said. "He's been helpful around the winery, put up with your father and uncle, and apologized to me for what his father did. And he's been honest since the beginning."

"Which I respect," my father added. "I respect a man who doesn't lie, even when the truth makes him despicable. He's never pretended to be something that he's not. Because of that reason, I'm willing to give him a chance. He and I aren't that different, unfortunately."

"I know you'll love him…in time," I said.

"I'd prefer it if you didn't tell him what your mother and I have agreed on," Father said. "I'd like to talk to him first."

It wouldn't be hard for me to keep that bottled inside since I couldn't talk to him anyway. "Okay. I hope that conversation ends with a handshake." Carmen was the only member of my family who had offered him the courtesy. Everyone else treated him like a criminal the day he set foot in our lives. I knew a handshake from my father would mean a lot to Bones after all the sacrifices he made.

My father didn't give any indication that it would. "We'll see."

TEN

Bones

It was a clean shot.

The bullet pierced the skull and exploded out the other end. The target was dead before he hit the ground. The hit took place in his hotel room, where he was waiting for his escort to show up. With a wife and two kids waiting at home, I thought killing him at this specific time would lessen the blow to his wife.

He was a pig. Now she could take his money and move on.

I finished the job and headed to my hotel. My flight didn't leave for six hours, and I hadn't slept since I'd arrived. I'd been too busy staking out the place and finding the perfect position to place the rifle. I also had to meet our guy here to collect the guns and ammunition I needed for the hit.

I was constantly on the go.

When I walked into my room, which had been

screened for cameras and microphones, I made the call to Max. "It's done."

"Where are you now?"

"In the room. I have six hours to kill before the flight. Thought I would get some sleep."

"You can fall asleep that quickly after killing someone?"

I never felt remorse for the things I did. My target was known for his fortune in jewelry, but the public didn't know they he had starving kids searching for diamonds in the most dangerous situations. Sometimes they made a few pennies for the day. He was a proponent of slave labor, pocketing millions in profit. Disgusting. "Yes."

Max didn't make another comment on the matter. "I think you should head to the airport now."

"Why?"

"I've already detected a lot of communications. His men are talking about him, and the police are looking for the killer because of his presence as a public figure. His brother is the one leading the hunt, and judging by their closeness, he's going to grab every lead he can find. If I were you, I wouldn't take any chances, not when you have a woman waiting for you."

"Is the threat that serious?"

"As far as I can tell, they have no idea who's behind it. But like I said, don't take the chance."

I hadn't slept in so long that I almost didn't care. But the mention of Vanessa, the woman who cried as she said goodbye, was heavy on my heart. I owed it to her to be overly cautious. If I died, she would die too. "Alright. I'll leave now." I grabbed my bag again and prepared to walk out.

"I checked on Vanessa the other day. Nothing to report. But she wanted me to pass on a message to you."

I halted in front of the door, thinking about the woman who filled my dreams. With that dark hair, beautiful skin, and soft-as-a-rose-petal lips, she was all I ever wanted. "What?"

"She said she loves you."

I already knew that, but the words touched me anyway. She wanted me to know how much she loved me, even if she couldn't hear me say it back. She was thinking about me every moment we were apart, desperate for me to come home. I told her not to ask me to quit...but knowing I was hurting her this much made me realize how impractical it was. I couldn't put my woman through this terror every time I left. I couldn't leave her unguarded while I was gone. She shouldn't have to stay with her parents because her man wasn't there to keep her safe. "Anything else?"

"Yeah. She said if you don't come back to her, she'll shoot you like she did last time."

I heard her sass and attitude even though Max was the one talking. That was the woman I fell in love with, bossy and aggressive. "Tell her I'm heading to the airport. I'll be back there in about twenty-four hours."

"Alright."

"And tell her I love her...and I won't leave her again."

235

I didn't know what would happen with her parents, but for as long as we were together, I couldn't do this anymore. I couldn't watch my woman cry every time I left. She'd turned me into a more compassionate man, made me feel emotions I'd turned off so long ago. I felt human again, felt vulnerable again.

Max was quiet, but he obviously knew the meaning behind my words. "I guess we'll have to talk about this in more detail when you get back…"

"Yeah. We will."

IT WAS MORNING when I arrived in Florence. My plane landed, and I took a cab to the house I shared with her. I didn't expect her to be there since she was probably at the winery for the day. As much as I wanted to see her, I was exhausted.

I needed sleep.

The cab pulled up to the gravel road, and I walked to the front door with my bag over my shoulder. My hand hadn't reached the doorknob before the front door was flung open and Vanessa stood there in a sexy ensemble— deep blue lingerie that was so sheer it was practically see-through.

Now I didn't feel so tired.

I shut the door behind me, dropped my bag on the hardwood floor, and then cupped her face with both my hands. My fingers dug into her hair and I kissed her as I cherished the woman I'd left behind. I felt like less of a man for leaving her alone, for not doing my job and keeping her safe.

"I'm here." I spoke against her mouth as I guided her backward down the hall. I wanted her on any piece of furniture I could find, whether it was the kitchen island or the couch. I settled for the wall and lifted her up, pinning her back against the plaster wall with her legs wrapped around my waist.

I kissed her neck and the valley between her tits, tasting a hint of olive that was ingrained in her blood. My hand fisted her hair, and I rocked into her, my hard cock rubbing against her through my jeans.

She pulled my shirt over my head then got my jeans loose so I could finally be free. My pants and boxers settled around my ankles, and my hard cock was finally against the lace of her bottoms.

I pulled them down her legs as I held her with a single arm. Her legs were so smooth and soft, luscious against my fingertips. I widened her thighs again and rubbed my length right against her aching clit.

She dragged her nails down my back as she moaned into my mouth. "Did you mean what you said?"

I guided the head of my cock to her entrance and slid inside, burrowing into the wet flesh that belonged to me exclusively. "Do I ever say anything I don't mean?" I held her in place, my hands under her ass and my cock fully sheathed. I watched her breathe through the stretching, watched her enjoy the way I made her feel.

"No…" She held on to my shoulders, full of me.

"Then you have your answer." I started to thrust inside her, my cock surrounded by her wetness. Her pussy was incredible, made just for me to enjoy. Boys may have had her, but they were never man enough to claim her like I did. I erased every man who had ever been there, claimed this territory as my own, and banished any other man from coming anywhere near her. She was mine.

Her fingers slid into the back of my hair. "Griffin…"

Vanessa erased the memory of every woman I'd ever been with. She made them seem insignificant, like they never happened in the first place. It didn't matter how beautiful they were. It didn't matter how sexy they were. They weren't this woman…the only woman who actually meant something to me.

She was the only woman who claimed my heart.

"Don't ever leave me again."

I thrust into her harder, hitting her back against the wall. "I won't."

"Promise me." She moved with me, her eyes fierce and emotional.

I grabbed her neck and looked her dead in the eye as I made love to her in the hallway. "I promise, baby."

I FELL asleep right after sex. I got into bed without showering, and I slept through the afternoon and all through the night. When I woke up the next day, Vanessa wasn't beside me. I smelled breakfast in the air and figured out where she ran off to.

I hopped into the shower first and got ready for the day before I joined her in the kitchen. She stood at the counter, a pile of burned pancakes sitting on a plate. Most of the bacon was burned too, with the exception of a few pieces.

When she noticed me, she set down the spatula and turned off the stove. "I was trying to make you breakfast...didn't work out too well."

I grabbed a piece of bacon and took a bite. "It's not bad."

"It's not good either."

I pressed her into the counter and kissed her. "It's the thought that counts."

Her hand moved across my flat stomach. "No. It's the fullness in my man's stomach that counts. I'm going to need to learn to cook so you don't starve to death."

"I can cook for myself, baby."

"But I want to cook for you..." She ran her hands up my chest, over my black ink, and looked into my eyes with self-pity. "Maybe Lars can teach me."

"Or I could teach you."

"You're busy."

"Not anymore." I hadn't had the formal conversation with Max, but he couldn't control my decisions. If I wanted out, that was the end of the story. There was nothing he could do to stop me.

She rested her forehead against my chest and sighed. "I hated having you gone...every second of it."

My palms moved up and down her arms, comforting her. "I know. When Max told me what you said...I knew I couldn't do it anymore. I don't want my woman staying at her parents' place because she's scared when I'm not there. I don't want to be that kind of man, a man who abandons his woman for cash."

"I've never felt abandoned, Griffin." She lifted her gaze to look at me. "I don't mind staying with my parents either. I don't mind missing you because it makes me appreciate you even more when you're here. Knowing you're in danger...that's what bothers me. That's why I can't sleep. That's why I feel scared." Her fingers snaked over my collarbone. "I wouldn't know what to do if I ever lost you..." Her eyes watered just thinking about it.

I cupped her face and brushed my thumb across her cheek. "You'll never lose me, baby. I'm right here—and I'm not going anywhere."

She wrapped her arms around my torso and rested her face against my chest. She hugged me tightly, her cheek cold against my warm chest. She held me in the middle of the kitchen, ignoring all the burned food she'd prepared for me.

My hand moved through her hair as I rested my chin on her head. "I love you." I kissed her hairline, smelling her shampoo and perfume. I had a beautiful woman in my arms, a woman who was strong and stubborn, but I'd managed to break her down until she loved me so deeply.

She turned weak for me, just the way I turned weak for her.

"I love you too." She lifted her gaze to look at me. "Let me make you a sandwich or something before you go since breakfast didn't work out."

"Where am I going?" I'd just traveled to the other side of the world. I had no interest in going down to the winery and moving crates all day, especially if I made the mistake of crossing paths with Carmen to initiate Cane's wrath. I loved spending my time with this petite woman in the privacy of my home. I didn't want to do anything else at the moment but be with her.

"To the winery."

I shook my head slightly. "No. I'm staying here with you. They can get someone else for labor."

Normally, Vanessa would be thrilled if I wanted to stay home with her and blow off everything else. But now she wore a timid expression. "I think you should go down there anyway."

I knew something was off because she would never try to talk me out of something. I was a stubborn man, and she couldn't change my mind unless it was for good reason. "What aren't you telling me?"

"My father wants to talk to you. That's all I'm going to say."

I grabbed her chin and directed her gaze on me, forcing her to lock her eyes on me. "Why?"

"Just go down there and find out."

"Why won't you just tell me? I'm about to walk into the snake pit, and you aren't giving me any warnings."

"He asked me not to say anything."

This continued to get stranger. "Vanessa."

She tried to look down.

I gripped her chin tighter. "Baby, tell me."

"I can't. But I will say this…it's a good thing."

My fingers loosened on her face, my eyes narrowed.

"Please go talk to him."

My heart started to beat hard in my chest, just the way it did before I killed someone. It was full of adrenaline, but it was also full of something similar to excitement, to hope. My blood pounded in my ears, and my breath came out quicker. I'd been working hard for this reward, but I wasn't sure if I would ever reap the benefits of my commitment.

Maybe it finally paid off.

I dropped my hand from her chin and turned away, focused on getting out of that house as quickly as possible so I could face her father.

And finally get his approval.

———

I PARKED my truck and then stepped inside the main building. Crow was probably in his office because that was where he spent most of his time. I checked in with his assistant, a woman his age, and then was escorted inside.

Crow didn't rise from his chair, and he had the same

irritated expression on his face that he always wore. His beard was gone because he'd shaved that morning, but his dark mysteriousness continued without it. Dark eyes accompanied by a clenched jaw, he stared at me like he hated me as much as he always had.

He rose out of the chair and grabbed a bottle of scotch and two glasses before he carried them to the coffee table. He set them down and took a seat.

I sat on the other side of the table, my arms resting on my knees and my fingertips together.

Crow poured two glasses and pushed one toward me.

It was only noon, but I knew Crow started drinking the second he finished his coffee. For a man who knew how to make the best wine in Italy, he still preferred the amber liquid of the finest scotch in Europe.

I took a drink while I kept my eyes on him, waiting for him to give a speech. Anytime he spoke to me, it felt like a threatening lecture. There were times when he wanted to kill me, but he somehow found the restraint. Based on what Vanessa said, this conversation seemed to be taking a new direction.

I did my best to stop my hands from shaking.

I'd never wanted something so much in my life. If I got to keep Vanessa, I would be happy for the rest of my days. I would leave the past behind me and become a new man. I would be a husband, and maybe I would be a father too.

Still, Crow said nothing.

I dropped my pride and spoke. "Vanessa said you wanted to talk."

"Yes. And I'll talk when I'm ready to talk." He grabbed his glass and took a drink, devouring half of it in a single gulp. His hands were corded with veins, as well as his forearms. His musculature resembled mine, except my muscle size was twice as big as his.

I could tell this was hard for him, and that told me my guess was correct. All my hard work was finally about to pay off.

"Vanessa said you quit. Is that true?" He set his glass down and stared at me, his eyes hostile even though the conversation was calm. His eyes shifted back and forth slightly as he looked at me, his fingers tight as they were clenched into two fists.

I didn't quit because he pressured me to. I did it because I wasn't going to make my woman cry every time I left. "Yes."

"For good?"

I nodded.

"What changed your mind? I haven't given you my approval."

I glanced at the glass sitting in front of me, half empty because I'd taken a big drink. Now I wanted more. I wanted the whole damn bottle. "She cried when I left. Then she told my handler to give me a message…that she loved me. It hit me hard in that moment. I was on the other side of the world, putting myself in danger and terrifying my woman, and she was here alone without me to protect her. I don't want her to stay with you every time I'm gone. She feels the safest with me...so I should be here. That was why I changed my mind."

Even though that was exactly what Crow wanted to hear, he still looked angry. "Took you long enough, huh?"

"It took you longer." The words flew out of my mouth before I could stop them. It was in my blood to retaliate anytime someone insulted me. I could keep my fist steady and not punch him in the face, but I couldn't sheathe my words as easily.

Crow grabbed his glass and finished it while he kept his eyes on me. He slammed it back down, the glass thudding against the cherry wood table. "Vanessa told me she's tired of waiting for my decision. So, she made it for me. My wife is on board with it too."

Finally. "I appreciate that."

"Keep in mind that I still don't like you. And I certainly don't trust you."

No surprise there. "That's fine."

"But I'm willing to accept you into our lives and try to like you...and trust you."

"That's very generous." Crow Barsetti used to be one of the most feared men in Italy. He didn't trust anyone, not after being molded by his horrible past. But he was willing to give this a try, because his love for his daughter outshone his doubts. "Thank you." I had to force those last words out, even though it burned my blood to do it. I shouldn't have to thank him for anything. I shouldn't even have to feel grateful. Vanessa was a grown-ass woman who could make her own decisions. Crow was acting like they were the royal family. But he was compromising with me, so I had compromised with him.

"Putting the past behind us would do us all some good. Maybe in the years to come…it could finally bring us all closure." He'd lost his sister, the woman he named his daughter after. And I'd lost my father.

It was the kind of stuff people never truly got over. "Yes…I agree."

He grabbed the bottle and refilled the glasses. "But before you walk out of here, there's something I've got to ask. I've come to respect your honesty and integrity, so I know you won't lie to me."

Fuck.

He stared me down, his hands together in between his knees. His hostility increased, burning the air around us both. His eyes smoked like a gun that just fired bullets. He seemed to anticipate my answer before I gave it, before he even asked the damn question.

He'd already asked me a hundred questions, even questions that were too personal between two strangers. If I were another man dating his daughter, he would never ask for the details that should be private between two adults. But in this scenario, he didn't seem to care.

So he could ask anything.

I finally found my voice, my heart beating a little faster. I was so close to having everything I wanted. He'd given me his permission, and I could go home to Vanessa right now and ask her to marry me. But her father kept me in place with his cold stare. "Alright." Despite the tremors rocking my body, I kept myself perfectly still. Perfectly fearless. I wasn't afraid of the man, just the power he had over me. He had the ability to change my future on a whim.

He massaged one knuckle with his other hand, his eyes trained on me. "Something in your story doesn't make sense to me. I'm not suggesting you're lying, but I think you left something out."

Fuck. Fuck. Fuck.

"Explain to me how my daughter fell in love with you. You kidnapped her, didn't kill her, still wanted to kill her whole family…and then what? You took her to dinner, and she agreed? I know my daughter. She's fierce and loyal. After everything you put her through, falling madly in love with you doesn't make sense. So tell me."

I held his gaze and felt my heart pound in my chest. The blood was loud in my ears. I could barely hear my own breathing because my distress blocked everything else out. The smart thing to do would be to lie, to lie to this man so I could have his daughter. I'd established enough credibility that I could probably get away with it. But it went against everything I believed in, to pretend to be something that I wasn't. I wanted to be accepted into this family, but only if they accepted me for everything that I was. "It didn't happen overnight. It took months for us to reach that level."

"I know. So how did you keep my daughter around all that time?"

He knew. He fucking knew.

"After everything you did to her, how did you keep her around?" His eyes narrowed further, drilling into my gaze.

"Crow, don't go there…"

"I already did." His jaw clenched. "I went through this story in my mind over and over. And then I remembered you said you fell in love with her and dropped your vendetta against us. But if that was months into this relationship, what happened before that moment? How were you connected to my daughter? Under what circumstances were you still seeing each other?"

"With all due respect, if I were another man, you wouldn't be asking such a personal—"

"Answer the fucking question." His nostrils flared.

Shit. I was about to lose everything.

"I wish you were another man. I wish you were a respectable man from a good family so I wouldn't have to ask these questions. I would know he treated my daughter with respect, took her to dinner, and earned her love. With you, I have no idea what the pretenses were. I have no idea if she ever would have loved you if the circumstances had been different. If she had a choice."

He didn't even need me to say it. He just wanted the truth out there so his actions would be justified. Maybe he planned to kill me. There was a gun sitting on his hip, fully loaded.

"Answer me. I'm giving you the opportunity to correct my assumption. Now, correct it."

I kept my mouth shut, refusing to lie even to save my

relationship with Vanessa. I had too much respect for my reputation, for being recognized as a man who always told the truth. That honesty got me here in the first place.

"How did it happen? Tell me."

I looked down at my hands for a moment, silently saying goodbye to everything I'd built with Vanessa. I'd imagined living in Florence with her, making love to her every morning before she went to her gallery in the city. I pictured adding ink to my body in her honor, getting a black ring tattooed on my left hand. I pictured myself having dinner with her family, five years down the line, and her father looked at me with kindness rather than hatred. But that beautiful vision was nothing but a dream. "I couldn't kill her because she deserved better. But I couldn't let her go either, not until I figured out what to do with her. So I told her I would spare her entire family…if she gave herself to me." I lifted my gaze again, looking him in the eye like a man. "And once she stopped, I would continue my vendetta."

Crow didn't react at first, his eyes unblinking and his gaze exactly the same. Slowly, the color started to come into his face, his olive skin reddening from the adrenaline that circulated through his heart. It seemed to take him a moment to process what I said, to absorb it to full capacity. It was the worst thing that a father could hear, that his daughter had to save her family by fucking me.

I wasn't sure if I would walk out of there alive. "We're in love now—"

"Shut. The. Fuck. Up." His hands balled into his fists,

and the vein emerged on his forehead. Throbbing and sporadic, it moved in time to his unpredictable behavior. He had so much rage but wasn't sure what to do with it. His breathing slowly increased, and the monster behind his eyes emerged.

He slowly rose to his feet, his hands by his sides. His arms were shaking, and his jaw was clenched so tightly he was about to break off a tooth.

I did the same, keeping myself at eye level at all times. I didn't know if I should prepare for battle or prepare to run. Regardless of what he did to me, I couldn't retaliate. I would never do that to Vanessa.

"This is over. Ends things with Vanessa and disappear."

No. A thousand knives pierced my lungs, and I couldn't breathe. My happiness was taken away so quickly, within the snap of a finger. "Sir." I raised both hands, unsure why I was even doing it. "I'm begging you, and I'm not the kind of man who begs. I love your daughter—"

He pulled the gun out of his holster and pointed it at my face within a second. His age didn't slow his speed. His draw was still good enough for the wild west. "I will shoot you, *Bones*. So get out before I do."

I slowly lowered my hands. "Sir, please."

He cocked the gun, his hand steady as he pointed the barrel at my face. "We made a deal. I tried, asshole. I really tried. But I will not let my daughter end up with a man who forced her—"

"I never forced her——"

He smashed the barrel of the gun into my face, making my nose and cheek bleed instantly. "You didn't treat her with the respect she deserves, and I will treat you exactly the same."

I slowly turned my face back to him, ignoring the bleeding and the swelling. "I would die for her——"

"I wish you were dead now." He pointed the gun at me again. "My daughter will marry a good man. She'll hate me for a while, but one day, she'll thank me for this. And when she finds the right one, she'll forget your name."

"She'll never love anyone the way she loves me."

His hand shook as he placed his finger over the trigger. "Leave. I won't shoot you now, but I'll save this bullet for later. If I ever see you again or anywhere near my daughter, I won't hesitate. I will put you in the ground, like the trash you are."

The fight left my body because I knew the war was over. Crow had made up his mind, and I'd just lost everything. I lost my woman and my future. Instantly, everything I cared about was taken away from me. "She'll be devastated."

"She'll get over it. She's a Barsetti. Barsettis aren't weak." He pressed the barrel right against my forehead, in between my eyes. "Now, go."

I stepped away, getting the cold metal off my forehead. I turned my back to him, not caring about exposing myself in the most vulnerable way possible. There was nothing that bullet could do to hurt me more than his decision had.

He might as well kill me.

I walked out of his office, feeling weaker by the second. He took away the only thing that mattered to me, and even though he was justified in his decision, I couldn't swallow it. I walked in there thinking the worst was finally over.

But it'd only just begun.